I0626273

MEGATOOTH
A DEEP SEA THRILLER

VIKTOR ZARKOV

SEVERED PRESS
HOBART TASMANIA

MEGATOOTH

WWW.SEVEREDPRESS.COM

ISBN: 978-1-925342-74-1

Megalodon, meaning "big tooth", from Ancient Greek: μέγας (megas) "big, mighty" and ὀδούς (odoús), "tooth"

1

Emily assumed that most twenty-three year-old single women came to Hawaii as a last exploration of single life. Maybe they came to stay on a resort with friends and meet an exotic single man. Or maybe they sat poolside with cocktails from ten in the morning until the sun went down. Perhaps they came to have those once-in-a-lifetimes adventures that were thick with self-discovery—adventures that were looked back on fondly in the years to come. And even for those not seeking romance, the beaches had their own allure, too; surely it was relaxing and nearly sensual to scrunch up your toes in sun-warmed sand right along the edge of where the ocean meets the land.

Emily had no idea about any of that. She was not in Hawaii to meet a man, live blissfully in a half-drunk state for a week, or to enjoy the beaches. Instead, she had come here from Minnesota, knowing that she'd only be on the land in Hawaii for about three hours. Her plane had landed in Lāna'i and she had promptly rented a car, driving across the small island to the hole-in-the-wall boat rental business that she currently looked at through her windshield.

She parked her car in the cracked lot and got out, getting her one lone suitcase out of the trunk. As she started across the lot of the wooden building that sat at the start of a pier that jutted out into the ocean, she saw three other cars in the lot. She recognized the face of the older man reaching into the trunk of his car at once. She had seen his face on various websites and in magazines. He was no celebrity…that was for sure. But Emily had been following his work since high school and admired the man considerably.

She veered away from her straight path towards the boat rental building and walked directly towards the man. He was still fumbling around with something in his trunk and seemed to be oblivious of the rather attractive twenty-three year old heading directly for him.

"Mr. Zinsser?" she asked as she neared his car.

"Yeah, that's me," he said, closing the trunk and looking at her. Seeing him this close, she saw that Cliff Zinsser actually looked a bit older than his thirty-six years. Apparently, his many years out on the ocean had taken its toll, the sun beating down on him and giving his skin an almost leathery appearance. Emily supposed the growth of hair on his face was supposed to look like a beard, but it looked sloppy and almost sporadic. His hair was disheveled and his clothes were dingy.

"I know," Cliff said. "Not much to look at."

"Oh, no," Emily said. "I was just—"

He smiled at her and waved the comment off. "I'm just kidding," he said. "Is this your first time out on a trip like this?"

"Yes, it is," Emily admitted.

"Well then, you'll understand the dress code in short order," he said. "Now, which one are you? I know there were two young women coming but I am terrible with names, so…"

"Emily," she said, extending her hand. "Emily Nevins."

"Nice to meet you. So, are you ready for this?"

"I am. I've been wanting to do something like this since my sophomore year of college."

"Good," he said. "It's always nice to see fresh, young blood getting involved in the good fight."

The *fight* was the struggle to bring justice to those that continued to poach sperm whales. As of late, there had been several reports of such heinous activity forty miles off of the coast of where she and Cliff Zinsser currently walked across a parking lot to a boat rental shop. It was a cause that Emily had cared deeply about since she had been in high school, but a fire had been lit under her in college that had nearly consumed her. She'd seen enough videos and documentaries…she'd had enough friends that had wanly turned their nose up at her desire to do something to help the environment and its endangered species. This was what she wanted to do with her life and she was anxious to get started.

She had just started grad school, with just a single semester under her belt. She knew the road ahead would involve some very hard classes and quite a bit of travelling. But she was in for all of that. After all, if she was going to sincerely make a go of it, what better way to start than to get involved in an expedition that might help bring a few poachers to justice? She knew it might be dangerous, but that was part of the appeal.

Well, that plus the fact that someone as well-respected in environmental circles as Cliff Zinsser was heading the trip up. The man wasn't much to look at, but something about the way he was so passionate about the cause had made Emily develop something of a crush on him a few years back. Now that she was standing next to him as they entered the rental shop, she felt that crush crumbling and transforming into something along the lines of pure respect. It was heartbreaking in a way but Emily couldn't remember the last time she'd had such an adult feeling about a man.

Cliff opened the door for her as they reached the front door of the rental cabin. Alongside the pier than connected the cabin to the ocean, several different boats were tied. They ranged from speed boats to what Emily assumed was a tug boat that had likely been in the water during the Biblical flood. When she stepped inside, Emily had her first true doubts about this trip. Suddenly, her often-frigid home in Minnesota seemed incredibly far away.

The shop smelled like bait, which made perfect sense as the place also sold several forms of it behind the counter. An elderly man in a clichéd-looking floral Hawaiian shirt greeted them with a nod and a mumbled, *"Aloha."*

"Aloha," Cliff said. "I believe you have a boat reserved under my name. Cliff Zinsser."

The clerk nodded and rummaged around under the counter. He retrieved a set of keys and handed them over to Cliff. "Can I please see your license and documentation?" the clerk asked.

Cliff removed the small backpack he was wearing and went looking for the materials. As he did this, Emily looked out of the window and back out to the parking lot. Another car was pulling in and when it pulled alongside her own rental, Emily knew who it was. She could barely see the shape of the driver, but she could see enough to know that it was Steve.

She frowned a bit, recalling the small bit of drama between them at the airport. She and Steve Locke had carpooled together for the trip from Minneapolis to Lānaʻi and then sat beside one another during the six-and-a-half hour flight. She knew Steve was very much into her and even though she had expressed no interest several times, he remained persistent. A large part of her was certain that the only reason Steve was on this expedition was to spend two days alone with her out at sea. Sure, it was a conceited thing to think about herself, but Steve made no attempts to hide any of it. Because of that, she had made a lame excuse at the rental car counter at the airport. She had insisted they get two cars because she wanted to do some sight-seeing when they returned and didn't want to hinder him. He had objected but she'd gone to the point of being rude to see that she got her own car.

The bad part of it was that Steve was an okay guy. If he didn't have what appeared to be an obsessive streak about him, Emily thought she could maybe convince herself to be interested in him.

When she saw him coming across the parking lot towards the rental shop, Emily stepped a bit closer to Cliff. She listened to Cliff and the clerk exchange a few pleasantries. With the key in his possession, Cliff gestured for the door.

"Shall we?" he asked.

She gave him a smile and left the shop. They had made it no more than five steps out towards the pier before Steve started coming in their direction. He stepped onto the pier, carrying a pack on his back and headphones hanging from his shoulders.

"You're Cliff Zinsser, right?" Steve asked.

"I am," Cliff said. "You must be... Steve, right?"

"That's me."

"Great. So glad you could join us!"

"Same here," Steve said, although he was sizing Cliff up in the same way a jealous dog eyes a visiting dog moments before it starts pissing everywhere to mark its territory.

"Well, we have one more coming with us," Cliff said.

"Yeah, that's Zoe," Emily said. "She's...well, she's *dedicated.*"

"That's an understatement," Cliff said. "When I spoke to her on the phone, she basically told me point blank that she wants in on this trip so it'll look good on her college applications. How did you manage to meet her?"

"College for a weekend," Emily said. "She stayed for the weekend as a visitor. She roomed with the girl that lives across the hall from me. She found out that I was majoring in Environmental Science and we started chatting. She e-mails me at least twice a week with articles she finds online about endangered species."

"She's looking to major in Marine Biology, right?" Cliff asked.

Emily shrugged. "That's what she said a few months ago. But she's only eighteen and straight out of high school. So we'll see if that changes or not."

"Speak of the devil," Steve said, nodding towards the parking lot.

They looked and saw another car turning in at a speed that was pretty close to reckless. As a group, they waited for the driver to get out of the car. Zoe Burton was listening to something rather loud on the rental's stereo and made no attempt to hide it. She got out in a flurry of movement, taking a pack out of the back of the car and quickly dashing across the lot to reach them.

"Why three cars?" Cliff asked as Zoe joined them. "That's not very economical."

"I've already been in Hawaii for two days," Zoe said. "Sort of a vacation with some friends." She took a moment to look around, as if she was just now realizing that she had arrived. "Hey guys." She then offered her hand to Cliff. "Zoe Burton," she said. "It's such a privilege to meet you, Mr. Zinsser."

Cliff took her hand and gave it a dainty shake. "Just Cliff, please."

"Sure," she said, nodding to Emily and Steve. She smiled widely at Steve, whom she had met a few times in preparation for the trip. Emily had even introduced them on one of the nights where Steve couldn't take a hint while Zoe was visiting, hoping he'd spring at the chance to impress an eighteen year old that was enamored with college men.

"We ready to go?" Zoe asked.

"Yup," Cliff said. "You guys load up, choose your bunks, and meet me in the main cabin in ten minutes. I'll run the necessary checks before we head out."

"Wait," Steve said. "You're driving? I thought we'd have like a pro driver or something."

"Yeah," Cliff said, giving him a comical look. "Nothing to fear… I've got more than fifteen years of experience. I've taken a boat out into these waters at least fifty times. You're in good hands."

"Okay," Steve said, but he still didn't seem convinced.

"Which boat is ours?" Emily asked, looking out to the boats alongside the pier again and thinking, *Please not the tugboat…*

"This one," Cliff said, pointing to his right to a small commercial vessel to their right. "It's not the best-looking thing, but it's great on fuel and has sleeping quarters for four down below."

Emily, Steve, and Zoe looked at the boat. Cliff was right; it wasn't much to look at. But it looked sturdy and well-used which, Emily guessed, was all that mattered. Navy blue letters had been painted along the back, dubbing the vessel *The Gull.*

Emily followed Cliff closely and then stepped on board. She felt the slight give of the boat on the water under her feet and was pleased to find that her heart was already leaping with excitement.

2

The boat actually looked a bit nicer once they were all on board. They all got on board at the back of the boat where Cliff instantly opened up a hatch and started looking at the engine. From the back of the boat, a single doorway allowed them into the cabin. Inside the cabin, there was a single table and a bench installed into the wall. A few cabinets and shelves lined the wall. Behind the table, two flights of stairs took up the rest of the cabin. One went up, clearly leading to the cockpit, and the other went down into a darkened area where four small rooms were set up.

Emily selected the first one she came to and when she stepped inside, she tried not to let the cramped space bother her. She barely had enough room to extend both of her arms. There was a small mattress with sheets on it, supported by a short metal frame. Other than that, the room was empty. She tossed her little suitcase on the bed and didn't bother to unpack. She went back up top to the back of the boat where Cliff was coming up out of the hull in which he had been checking on the engine.

"Everything looks good from my end," Cliff told her. "You all settled?"

"The rooms are pretty small," she said. "There's not much to get settled."

"So you understand what I was talking about in terms of the dress code?"

"I'm starting to," she said.

Steve and Zoe came up the stairs and out of the cabin behind her. Zoe was looking out to the ocean as if she didn't totally trust it while Steve stood directly beside Emily. He looked to her like a child that was waiting on instructions from its favorite parent.

Sensing the hesitation in his young and inexperienced crew, Cliff pointed up to the cockpit. "I've got a few more things to check out. Head up there and I'll be up in about five minutes. Look around and let me know if you have any questions. We're going to get to know each other very well over the next two days—maybe a little *too* well—and I want to make sure you three are as well-informed as you can be."

With that, Cliff walked back onto the pier and headed to the rental cabin again. Emily, still very much enamored over being in the presence of Cliff Zinsser, went dutifully back into the cabin and headed up the stairs to the cockpit. Unsurprisingly, Steve went directly after her. Zoe brought up the rear, trailing behind in a way that made it clear that she felt out of place.

"You getting excited?" Steve asked. He asked in a tone that Emily had come to know all too well. It was one that was desperate for a conversation and once again reminded her of that downtrodden child that was looking for approval from a parent. She resented him for coming on this trip because he was going to be doing it the whole time—she just knew it. Why would the next three day be any different than the past eight months?

Still, she was determined to not let Steve ruin this for her. She could tolerate him and still get something out of this trip. Hell, maybe he would go back home with an actual appreciation of their cause. Maybe he'd better understand the severity of what was happening to the sperm whale population. Maybe he'd start to care about something other than trying to talk her into dating him.

"Yeah, a little," she said. "Nervous, too."

She glanced around the cockpit and was relieved to see that the controls and equipment were in much better shape than the outside of the boat had led her to believe. She knew what very little of the equipment did and was not going to fake an interest by asking pointless questions. She knew that Cliff had a stellar reputation for these sorts of expeditions and that he was also incredibly skilled out in open water. She was in good hands and that knowledge was enough reassurance as far as she was concerned.

"Okay," Zoe said. "Confession time. I'm sort of scared out of my mind."

"Why?" Steve asked. "You never been on a boat before?"

"No, I have. On a lake for skiing. Not out in the middle of the ocean where you can't see land. How about you guys?"

"I went on a cruise with my parents when I was in middle school," Steve said.

"And I've been about six miles off the coast of North Carolina for a dolphin sight-seeing sort of thing," Emily said.

Zoe nodded but still seemed freaked out. "We'll be okay, right? I've read tons about Mr. Zinsser and he seems reputable out on the water."

"Absolutely," Emily said. She could go on and on about all of Cliff's qualifications, but she didn't want to come off as being a kiss-ass.

"Okay," Zoe said hesitantly. She eyed the controls and electronics of the cockpit with reservation. She reached out and touched the helm, giving the wheel a nervous caress.

"So here's the question I have," Steve said. "Let's say we find some of these poachers. What do we do then? I don't think three college-aged kids and an environmental activist are going to really scare them off."

Their answer came from behind them as Cliff bounded up the stairs with two duffel bags. "We keep our distance," he said. "We take pictures of the vessel—with identifying marks or tags, if possible—and mark down the coordinates. I'll then radio those in to the Institute of Cetacean Research. They'll have someone within their agency send someone out to take care of the legal part."

"Have you done this before?" Zoe asked.

"About a dozen times. Most recently, I was on an expedition off the coast of Japan and we were able to locate eight poaching vessels. Within a week, more than twenty men were arrested and fined."

"Awesome," Zoe said, smiling. Emily saw the same passion in Zoe's eyes that had once been in her own when it came to the topic of poaching and endangered species in general. Seeing this made the nerves go away, replaced by an urgency to get out on the water.

"So, guys," Cliff said, kicking at the duffel bags he'd brought up. "I'll be kicking us off here in a few minutes. In these bags you'll find all of the food and supplies we'll need for the next two days. If you would, please set it all up as you see fit. Also, no fighting over the food…not that there's much to choose from. I hope you like cereal and peanut butter and jelly."

Emily couldn't help but notice the look of worry on Steve's face. She suspected that he hadn't taken the time to read over everything this trip entailed. Between the cramped sleeping quarters, the lack of food, and the uneventful hours on the open sea, she had a feeling that Steve might be resenting this trip as early as tomorrow morning. A small part of her was almost flattered that he would take part in such a thing just to be alone with her—especially if it made him this uncomfortable. Sure, it was borderline creepy, but the attention was nice. It wasn't like she had guys knocking down her door for a chance to spend time with her.

Emily took one of the bags and, eager to please, Steve took the other one. They went down to the small central area of the cabin and started filling the cabinets and shelves with the food. There were crackers, Cheerios, a few loaves of bread, peanut butter, jelly, a pack of pudding cups, a case of bottled water, and a case of Gatorade.

"Not much like the cruise you went on with your folks, huh?" Zoe asked Steve as she came down the stairs.

"No, not at all," Steve said, making no effort to hide his annoyance.

As he hunched over his bag, Zoe gave Emily a smile and a roll of the eyes. Emily nodded her agreement and appreciation and continued to unpack.

3

Thirty-six miles away from where Cliff Zinsser was about to take three students out on their first open-sea adventure, three men were undergoing their own adventure. They were on a boat that was not too dissimilar to the one that Cliff and his crew had rented, only theirs did not come from a rental shop. Their boat was owned and maintained by a small yet relatively wealthy company called MarineEx. Only a handful of people knew the vessel was on the water and not all of those selected few even knew why the crew was out there.

Carl Peters knew, though. As he walked along the deck of the boat and looked out to the ocean, he stared with hope. To his right, coming off of a mechanical device that he barely understood, a large metal tube extended outward, took a sharp angle, and then plummeted into the water. The device beside him, which was really nothing more than a glorified super pump, made a constant humming noise that reminded him of the old crappy air conditioning unit he'd had in his first apartment.

The device was hooked into a monitoring system that was installed in the cabin, being watched over by Trevor Thomas, an irritable man that rarely came out of the cabin. In the course of the three days they'd been out at sea, Trevor had come out of the cabin only four times and had not spoken unless spoken to. That was fine with Carl. Trevor was in the middle of a nasty divorce and wasn't exactly the most cheerful person in the world to talk to.

Still, the only other person on the boat was a man named Bo— a Korean engineer that had the humor and personality of roadkill.

He was strictly business-minded and there was something about him that brought out the mean jock in both Carl and Trevor— even though neither of them had been jocks in high school. Bo had a last name that was almost impossible to pronounce, so both Carl and Trevor had stopped trying and he had always simply been "Bo" to them.

So in terms of having people to break up the monotony of this experimental trip, there was no one. Carl felt like he was stranded, taking part in some weird social experiment.

True, the purpose of their journey *was* experimental in a way. They were out here performing a very cutting edge and controversial form of deep ocean mining. It was really just a research trip more than anything, a way to see if the overpriced set-up that they were carrying on board would actually work. If it *did* work, Carl knew that he would get a very nice paycheck soon after they returned to land. And if it *didn't* work, then they'd be back out here again within six weeks for a third attempt. And that would be fine with Trevor; it would give him more time to tinker with the rovers that were currently investigating the ocean floor beneath them.

As Carl looked out to the clear skies and the calm seas, he heard footsteps coming around the corner of the cabin. He found it hard to believe that Trevor had come out of the cabin and abandoned his precious equipment, so he assumed it was Bo. He turned around to find that he was correct.

"How are ya?" Carl asked.

"Okay," Bo said. "I'd be better if we were getting more results."

"Same here," Carl said. "I do *not* want to end up back out here six weeks from now."

"Can we not get an extension on our stay this time?" Bo asked.

"No. The latest we can return tomorrow is seven in the afternoon."

"That's no good," Bo said and walked over to the large metal extension. He glanced at it like a hopeful child before turning his head to the east. "When should we relocate?" he asked.

"Let's give it another hour here," Carl said. "Then we'll move on."

"Sounds good," Bo said. "I'll tell Trevor."

Better you than me, Carl thought.

With Bo gone, Carl returned his attention to the pump-device that looked nothing like a pump but rather some abstract upside down ventilation pipe from a wood stove. Although Carl was the supervisor of the small crew, he knew the least about the equipment but he had at least a fundamental understanding of what the mining equipment was supposed to do. All he knew was that his head was the one that would roll if anything happened to any of this expensive and experimental crap.

The large tube-like thing attached to the boat and plunged into the water was a hybrid of a basic pump (although a high-powered one) and a souped-up metal detector. The detector was under water, attached to the pump and suction device via a tether that Bo could remotely operate and keep tabs on. This pump was referred to as The Collector, namely because the actual terminology MarineEx had applied to it was overly complicated.

As a crew, they used Trevor's surveying equipment to locate large pockets of polymetallic nodules and hydrothermal vents. These locations were usually rich in sulfide deposits—prime targets for copper, manganese, silver, and gold.

Once the detector—which looked like a miniaturized version of the Mars Rover, minus the treads—picked up one of these deposits, they would submerge six rovers down below. Each rover was built just like the detector, only much bigger. The size of a small car, each rover was equipped with blades and drills that could be remotely directed to cut and clear away debris and seabed from any direction. These were the auxiliary cutters and were the most expensive part of their set-up. Once the cutters were in business, the pump—the Collector—was turned on and anything of note was brought to the boat and dumped into the device's filtration system. The filtration system then sorted the useless debris from the precious treasure.

So far, there was very little precious treasure to be found. This was not good, especially considering that they were currently perched high above several large sulfide deposits. Carl didn't have an exact figure, but he was pretty sure this one trek alone was costing MarineEx about $250,000—not to mention the fifteen million they had spent on the rovers and the pump system.

Coming back with no reason to be excited could be disastrous. Sure, they'd just send him back out in a few weeks, but he wasn't sure how long they would keep sending him out if he came back without results. And while these trips were boring and monotonous, he also knew that his job could be on the line.

He heard another set of footsteps, these much harder and pronounced than Bo's. He looked to his right and saw Trevor come walking down the thin walkway between the pump and the cabin. Carl didn't even have time to make a smart-assed comment about the bear coming out of hibernation before Trevor started with his inane questions. He never seemed to run out of dumb unanswerable questions and now was no different.

"Are you kidding me with this tomorrow afternoon stuff?" Trevor asked as he neared Carl. "You can't get them to push it?"

"No," Carl said. "We've already talked about this."

"Yes, but how in the hell am I supposed to work the kinks out in my software and formulas if we keep coming and going in four day increments?"

"Why are you just now asking me these things?" Carl asked, now attacking with his own questions.

"Because the detectors are doing better than I expected. Sure, they aren't really finding much of anything, but they're performing spectacularly. And the Collector is pulling with more strength and accuracy than I had hoped."

"That's great," Carl said. "Write a report stating as much and maybe they'll consider giving you some extra time the next time we come out."

Trevor gave him a scowl and shook his head in frustration. "Just call and ask, man."

"It's no use," Carl said. "They won't change it."

"And you don't want to upset them. Is that right?"

"That *is* right," Carl said. "We're going back with very little results. I'd like to find as few other reasons as possible to piss them off even more."

Trevor fumed and looked out to sea. He shook his head and gave a condescending little laugh. "We work for idiots. You know that, right? I know they're afraid it might cost them some unexpected expense to stay out here another day or so. But they can't see past their fat wallets to understand that they'd be saving money in the long run if they just let us run the show out here."

Carl actually agreed with this line of thinking, but there was no way he was going to let Trevor know that. "Well, I can pass that message along if you'd like," he said, trying to get his point across without being confrontational.

"Whatever," Trevor said, storming away. "I guess I'd better make use of the little bit of time I *do* have."

Carl sighed and looked to the pump again. When he did, he saw something bobbing up out of the water roughly forty feet away from the boat. It glistened in the late morning light but it was hard to tell what it was—the sheen of it and the way it moved almost playfully in the water made him think it was a dolphin.

He glanced out, focusing on that area and saw it again. When he saw it this time, he realized that the object wasn't bobbing at all. It was being moved by the water, its motionless shape being pushed by the idle surface of the water. The water moved it slowly, bringing it closer to the boat.

It took only a few moments for Carl to piece together the fact that what he was seeing was a dead fish of some sort—a very large fish, at that. Maybe he had been right to assume it had been a dolphin in the first place. It seemed to have a light grey skin, although the sunlight and the movement of the water made it hard to see clearly.

Curious, he turned towards the cabin, wanting to grab his binoculars from his quarters. When he did, he saw Bo coming back around the corner.

"Everything okay?" Carl asked, surprised to see Bo again so soon.

"Yes. I was up top, wasting time, honestly. I looked out to sea and saw that," he said, pointing to where Carl had been looking moments ago.

"I saw that, too," Carl said. "I was just heading in to get my binoculars."

"It's a sperm whale," Bo said. "I'm fairly certain."

"Yeah?" Carl asked.

"I think so. There are waters out this way that are popular with poachers."

"Why would people poach sperm whales?" Carl asked.

Bo only shrugged. "It's a shame, though. They are beautiful creatures."

Then, as if he had just laid down some profound knowledge, Bo walked to the rail and looked out to the dead whale somberly. Carl looked back out to, his binoculars temporarily forgotten. As the water drew the whale closer, he started to get a real idea of the thing's size. It was a massive creature and something about it being dead didn't quite seem right. He found it hard to imagine a human being killing such a thing—not because he thought humans were incapable of such cruelty (he knew they were), but because the thing was just so damned big.

He joined Bo, looking out to the whale as it came closer and closer. Beside him, the pump hummed on, all business as usual. Carl eyed the whale, its grey hide now clear and almost shimmering in the play of sunlight on the water. He felt bad for the creature but, at the same time, was reminded just how large the sea was and how many unseen horrors took place on its waters.

He also scanned the horizon for other boats, wondering if they might find themselves in danger if a poacher ship *did* show up. But the horizon was clear and the waters were calm and almost pristine. Still, something about the dead whale approaching their boat unnerved him and no matter how hard he focused on the formulaic hum of the pump beside him, he could not shake it.

4

Two hours into their trip, Cliff brought the boat to a stop. The engine puttered while they were pushed along by the waves. He called his crew of three up while he looked out to the water through the windows of the bridge.

Emily heard the call from the back of the ship where she had been sitting in a trance-like state, watching the ocean unravel behind her. At Cliff's instruction, she got up right away. Wondering if they had already found a poaching vessel, she grew excited as she went into the cabin and up the stairs to the bridge.

Zoe was already on her way up the stairs, eager to please. Emily was well aware of Steve coming up the stairs behind her and she could practically feel his eyes on her rear as she climbed up. A shudder passed through her but she managed to shrug it off when she was in the bridge and looking straight ahead.

"So, this is a recent hot spot," Cliff said. "Less than two weeks ago, most of my sources agree that at least two poaching vessels were spotted in these waters. We know that minke whales and sperm whales are often targeted in these areas. So what I need you guys to do is to keep your eyes peeled for the next few hours. Take posts along the boat and let me know right away if you see any other boats."

"Excuse me for asking," Steve said, "but what are we supposed to do if we come across poachers? We can't exactly scare them away."

"You're right," Cliff said. "But we can take their information and call it in, like I already said. Officials will be out within a few hours. As I said before, it's not our job to stop the poachers, but to turn them in and see to it that they pay for what they have done."

Steve said nothing; he just looked out to the ocean as if he had just found something of interest out there. It was clear that he was bored, annoyed, and really didn't want to be there. Emily was furious with him and it took every ounce of energy within her not to snap at him. Was he seriously trying to purposefully get on the bad side of the man that was leading this expedition? She was relieved to see that Cliff already seemed to be getting fed up with it, too.

"Son, why are you even here?" Cliff asked.

Emily knew the answer but didn't dare say it at the risk of sounding conceited. Besides…she wanted to see what answer Steve could come up with. She was surprised at how blunt the question was. Cliff had never struck her as the confrontational type.

"To help protect the whales," Steve said, trying his best to feign hurt feelings.

"Yeah?" Cliff asked. "What's your major?"

"Journalism."

Cliff made a *hmmm* sound and then shrugged. "I get the feeling you aren't here with the same passion as these two young ladies," he said. "I hope I'm wrong about that."

"You are," Steve said, now practically fuming. He took a few steps toward the stairs leading back down into the central cabin but was halted by more comments from Cliff.

"That's good," Cliff said. Emily could hear the anger in his voice and was reminded of the passion this man had not just for sperm whales, but other endangered oceanic species as well. "Because I wouldn't want to waste your time out here if you weren't well-informed about the horrific deaths these whales endure at the hands of far too many asshole humans. That would include being harpooned numerous times with explosives and then drug behind vessels until it's brought up to the main boat and then shot several times with a high-powered rifle. They're shot in the stomach with those explosive harpoons and as if that's not torture enough, they are then dragged for miles, suffering and bleeding across the sea—across their home. And that's *after* they've been hunted and chased to the point of exhaustion."

"I didn't ask for a—" Steve started to say, but Cliff was on a roll and would not be interrupted.

"What happens to them out here on these waters is so bad that even whaling insiders have said that if whales had any way to scream, the whaling industry would have closed up shop a long time ago."

Steve stood there for a moment, his mouth simply hanging open as if a word or two planned to spill out. After a few awkward seconds, though, he closed it and just walked down the stairs.

When he was gone, Cliff turned to Emily and Zoe with a slightly embarrassed look on his face. "Sorry about that," he said.

"No problem," Emily said. "I think you were justified."

"You guys know him pretty well?"

"Not me," Zoe said.

"I do," Emily said with a frown. "And yeah, his reasons for being here might not exactly be the right ones."

"How so?" Cliff asked.

Emily shrugged, trying to think of the right way to say it. As it turned out, though, she was able to sidestep the question. A static-laced squeal came from the radio behind Cliff.

"Zinsser, you there?" a voice asked through the hiss and crackle of radio static.

Cliff picked up the small mic and responded while fiddling with the controls on the radio. "Yeah, I'm here. Who is this?"

"It's Harper," came the voice again, clearer this time now that Cliff had fine-tuned the signal. "I've got a tip…maybe not the best and surely not a certified source, but maybe worth checking out since you're already out that way."

"Sure thing," Cliff said. "What have you got?"

"We've got reports of an undocumented ship out your way…to the west of where you are."

"How far out?" Cliff asked.

"We don't have any real intel," Harper said. "Maybe about ten or twenty miles."

"Where'd the information come from?"

"Some internet geek."

"Sounds promising."

"I know. Check it out if you want. Never hurts, you know?"

"Yeah, we'll head to the west, then," Cliff said.

"Fill me in when you get there," Harper said.

"Will do. Out."

Cliff hung the mic up and kicked the boat back into hear. There was a noticeable surge forward as the boat started moving again, heading west this time.

"Who was that?" Emily asked.

"A friend of mine," Cliff said. "I texted him this boat's channels just before we left. He sort of works in the background for me, scouring message boards, forums, Reddit, and every other black hole of the internet where people try to keep tabs on illegal whaling practices."

"Oh," Emily said, suddenly a little uncomfortable with just how shady and determined Cliff seemed to be. "That doesn't sound very official."

Cliff laughed. "Yeah, it really doesn't. But it's the quickest way to get information these days. Think about it. Because of Twitter, you can get real-time news within about twenty seconds of it happening. Meanwhile, other news outlets are hauling ass just to be the first to get it to the air in about five minutes. It's the same way collecting info out here."

"That's pretty cool," Zoe said, seemingly not affected by it at all. "It's sort of like an underground network of spies."

Cliff shrugged. "I guess so," he said. "Now, if you ladies don't mind, take posts down below and help keep an eye out. If you see anything, don't yell…sound carries very weirdly out here over the water sometimes. Come on up and tell me. And above all, remember…don't be scared. I've done this a dozen or so time and I've never even come close to getting into an altercation of any kind with the vessels I turn in."

Emily and Zoe headed down the stairs and back out onto the open spaces of the boat. Now that it seemed they might be on the brink of finding a poaching vessel, Emily truly started to worry about the potential dangers. Even with Cliff assuring her that all was well, it was hard to truly believe it. With no land in sight and only ocean to all sides, she was beginning to understand just how isolated and alone they were out here.

"Hey, Zoe," Emily said. "The whole *'hey, some dude on the internet thinks there might be a boat out your way'* thing...did that creep you out a little bit?"

"Maybe a little," Zoe admitted. "But to be honest, I really wasn't sure what to expect from all of this anyway."

Same here, Emily thought. *But it certainly wasn't anything like this.* She had been expecting the renowned cliff Zinsser to be very organized and cautious—not the type to take tips from nobodies on the internet. Then again, the man's track record spoke for itself.

She took her post to the rear of the boat while Zoe walked to the front. As Emily stood there, she caught a flicker of motion to her left. She saw Steven slowly pacing around the boat as if he were looking for a way to escape. Their eyes locked for a brief moment and something about the look in his eyes almost made her feel bad for him. It was evident that he did not want to be here. And while he carried the appearance of a school yard bully that had finally gotten his feelings hurt, there was something else there, too.

Is he scared? It was a humbling thought and made him seem a little more relatable but Emily was too preoccupied with her own worries to really care.

She looked away, her eyes once again back out to the water. She listened to Steve pass behind her and then head back to the front of the boat to finish his circuit. Emily closed her eyes for a moment and took a deep breath, suddenly wishing she'd stayed in Minnesota.

5

"I had no idea these things were so ugly," Trevor said, squeezing in next to Carl to get a better look.

The whale was now within ten feet of their boat and had taken a slight path to the right, fortunately missing their pump by a good fifteen yards. It was easily over fifty feet long; its head was directly beside their boat while its tail was further out behind them, barely visible as it was curled lifelessly just beneath the water. Carl, Trevor and Bo were all standing at the back of the boat, looking at the dead whale. Its right side was above the water, one large dead eye looking at them.

But its eye wasn't what Carl was paying attention to. What was of particular interest to him was the bloody mess along the center of the whale's body. It was mostly hidden by the water, but it was clear that the whale had been seriously injured. It looked like a large portion of its underside had been torn open and, if Carl was assuming correctly, the wound came all the way around to the side that was currently exposed to the air.

"That's pretty gruesome," Bo said. "Poachers, you think?"

"That's my guess," Carl said. "Aren't sperm whales supposed to be the biggest creature in the ocean?"

"I think that's blue whales," Bo said.

"What about giant squids?" Trevor asked. Sadly, Carl couldn't tell if he was trying to be funny or if it was a legitimate question. When it was clear that neither Carl nor Bo were going to address this, Trevor added: "I wish we could turn it over somehow."

"What for?" Carl asked.

"That's a big wound," he said. "If poachers did that, they were either sloppy with their work or just really like inflicting abuse."

"You think it was attacked by something?" Bo asked.

Carl looked to the part of the wound that was visible above the water. Though he hated to admit it, Trevor was right. The portion of the wound that they could see was ragged and looked enormous—it took up about half of the whale's length. The skin had been shredded and flayed in a violent manner, tearing through the hide and revealing the tissue beneath. Carl assumed it was much worse beneath the water.

"I'm pretty sure there's nothing out there that could do that sort of damage," Carl said. "Even a great white…there's no way in hell a great white's mouth is that wide."

"Well," Trevor said, "I can't help but wonder…"

Carl wondered if he was pausing for dramatic effect or if he was really thinking. With Trevor, it was always hard to tell. He sometimes did things for the sole purpose of getting on people's nerves.

"You wonder what?" Bo asked.

"I'm getting a lot of debris on the ocean floor, even before I switch on the rovers. It's been screwing with my readings for the last day or so. Maybe there *is* a shark or something down there that did this."

"That's unlikely," Bo said. "Now, maybe if it was like a group of sharks working together…"

"Do they do that?" Carl asked.

"I don't know," Bo said.

"Me neither," Trevor said. "Outside of *Jaws*, I know squat about sharks."

Carl looked back to the whale and then further out to the water. Something about being this close to the whale sort of creeped him out. He looked to the pump and frowned.

"Trevor, I need you to shut the pump down. Retract it and bring the ROVs up. Let's move another half a mile forward."

"But we've got another hour or so here. I've already programmed it in. And bringing those rovers up, locking them down, and then submerging them again is about a half an hour wasted."

"I understand that," Carl said. "But I need you to do it anyway. We're moving."

Trevor gave a heavy sigh but said nothing. He gave the whale one more cursory look and headed into the galley. Looking at this reaction, Carl wondered how much longer he'd be able to work with Trevor before they came to blows. When Trevor got pissed off (which seemed to be most of the time these days), there was a tangible tension between them. Trevor had issues with anyone giving him orders and maybe rightly so; he was incredibly smart and his engineering degrees probably trumped the little bit of college that Carl had under his belt. But none of that mattered on this little journey out to sea. Out here, Carl called the shots regardless of qualifications, and it got under Trevor's skin.

"Sort of scary, isn't it?" Bo asked after Trevor was out of hearing range.

"What do you mean?" Carl asked.

"To think that there could be something out there that could give this massive whale such a beating."

"Yeah," Carl said. He then recalled a story in the news a few years back about how some giant squid had been found near Japan. At the time, it had been believed to be the largest creature in the ocean, rivaling the sea monsters that had been reported during pre-Colonial times. Carl also knew that there were undiscovered depths in the ocean where God only knew what sorts of things existed.

He looked away from the whale when he heard the vacuum within the pump shut down. This was followed by a hissing noise as the pump was raised, folding up on itself as Trevor retracted it from the main controls. The Collector was an independent piece of the pump and would come up with the ROVs, jettisoned up through the water by small but effective air boosters along the bottom of each rover. While he waited for all of this to play out, Carl went back inside and headed up to the bridge.

He peered in at Trevor and saw that he looked absolutely pissed to be moving away from the area earlier than planned, but didn't let it bother him. Trevor was *usually* pissed off about something so it was nothing new.

"You said yourself that there's been too much debris," Carl said. "I figure if we move away from this dead whale and whatever might have happened to it, we'll get better results."

Trevor gave a mock shrug and an exaggerated smile. "Hey man, it's cool. You're the boss. Just tell me what you want done."

Carl didn't even bother with a sarcastic "Thanks." He scurried past Trevor's small corner set-up where the pump and other mining equipment were installed and operated and continued on to the bridge. When he started the engine and waited for Trevor to give the go-ahead, he looked out to the ocean, and, not for the first time since starting his career out on the seas, was awestruck by it.

There were innumerable creatures in its depths, some of which had not yet even been spied by human eyes. He often lost himself in wondering what sort of mysteries might be down there. He did that now, staring blankly out to sea and wondering what sort of unnamed beast could have possible taken down that poor sperm whale.

6

Emily Nevins was also beginning to feel restless as a creeping uneasiness started to settle on her nerves. She had been so wrapped up in the idea of potentially saving the lives of the whales that she hadn't taken the time to consider how they would be doing it. Her mind ran rampant with visions of modern day pirates like in that Tom Hanks movie *Captain Phillips*. After all, if a man had no problems with ruthlessly killing an endangered whale, why would he have an issue with putting a bullet in the brain of a clueless yet motivated grad student from Minnesota?

Thinking back on it, she supposed all of the warning signs had been there, clear as a bell. She knew a few other students that had been invited on trips like this—usually for actual studying and research—by professors or connections made through professors. Emily had always envied the students that had been selected for such trips so when she had received the e-mail from Cliff Zinsser's personal assistant, she had jumped at the chance to be a part of this trip. It had seemed a little too good to be true at first, so she had done some very basic research. She had Googled the name of the assistant (Monica Denbrough) and that checked out. She also saw on Cliff's blog that he had a few trips planned for the remainder of the summer, so that checked out as well. When she had called the number given in the e-mail, it had skipped Monica Denbrough and had gone directly to Cliff. She'd been too elated to even care, much less assume that something underhanded was going on.

Even now, looking out for potential poacher vessels like some poorly trained mercenary, Emily wasn't entirely convinced that something about this trek smelled a little fishy (terrible pun not intended). She had no experience with these sorts of trips; her only knowledge came from a few shows she'd seen on The Discovery Channel and a handful of articles she'd read online.

Something about the easy nature in which she'd been invited seemed odd at best and she started to wonder just how trustworthy Cliff was. Sure, he'd done nothing to make her think ill of him so far and as far as people within nature conservation circles were concerned, the man was a saint. Maybe she was now seeing some sort of secret underbelly to what Cliff and others like him did. Maybe he had to be just as covert as the people he was trying to stop on occasion. What confused Emily, though, was why this made her think less of him rather than painting him as a hero.

As if he was aware that she was thinking such things, his voice sounded out from behind her.

"Emily, come here for a second," he said, poking his head out of the upper cabin window where he remained on the bridge.

She went willingly enough—anything to get her eyes off of the water and the horizon behind them. She had no idea how she would react if they *did* happen to come upon a poacher ship. She figured she'd probably just freak out and let her nerves take over. *Steven would love that,* she thought. *It would give him a chance to come running in to my rescue.*

She climbed the cabin stairs into the bridge, wondering where Steven was now. If she was lucky, perhaps he was striking up a conversation with Zoe and relocating his borderline-stalker interests.

When she reached the bridge, she found Cliff very excited. He was looking at the instrumentation panel and leaning from left to right in an anxious sort of lazy dance.

"What is it?" Emily asked. She was pleased to find that her feelings of unease started to fade in the presence of his excitement.

Cliff pointed to the depth finder. "Right there," he said. "See that?"

She gazed to the spot where his finger hovered and saw a rather large dot on the blue screen. There were other dots here and there, but the dot Cliff was pointing to dwarfed them; the smaller ones were the size of pepper flakes while the larger one was the size of a peanut.

"I see it," she said.

"That's one of our friends," he said. "Definitely a whale…and of that size, I'm guessing a blue."

"Really?" she asked, her own excitement now growing.

"I'm almost positive. This is a big one, too. Being so close to us, if we keep our eyes peeled, we might see it surface for a bit. It's a crapshoot, really."

"Awesome," she said. "Let me go tell the others."

"Sounds good," Cliff said. "And when you tell Steve, if you want to give him a hard shove overboard, I won't tell anyone."

"Don't tempt me," she said as she started bouncing her way down the stairs.

Back out in the open air, the sea around her now seemed more exciting than ever. She looked to her right, where the depth finder had indicated the whale would was swimming, and saw nothing of note. Still, there was a spring in her step as she approached Zoe, standing along the port side of the ship.

Zoe looked away from the water and gave her a smile. "I'm beginning to think I am not cut out for a life at sea," she said.

"Same here," Emily said. "But Cliff just showed me something on the depth finder." She pointed out to the direction where she imagined the whale should be, swimming deep below them. "Somewhere over there, a very large fish is swimming. Cliff says it's so big that it almost *has* to be a blue whale."

Zoe instantly started digging into her back pocket for her iPhone. In a motion so slick and practiced that it made her look like a machine, Zoe opened her camera and readied it.

"We may not actually get to see it," Emily said, hating to rain on the parade.

"See what?" came Steven's voice from behind them.

"Blue whale," Zoe said.

"Yeah?" he asked, mildly interested. "How do you know?"

"I saw it on the depth finder," Emily said.

"With Cliff?" he asked.

Emily rolled her eyes and didn't bother responding. She looked back out to the water expectantly. As she did, she noticed a darkening of the sky towards the horizon. Somewhere ahead of them was about to get rain, or so it seemed.

"I don't see anything," Steven said.

"Well, they *do* live underwater," Emily said. "They don't just swim up to the surface when people are overhead. It has no idea we're here. We might get lucky, though and—"

"Hey guys!" Cliff's head was out of the window again. "Go up front and get a look...up ahead and slightly to the left. It's getting close and its coming up...looks like it might breach. I think we might have a show on our hands!"

Zoe responded immediately, rushing to the front of the boat. Emily smiled as she watched her go, remembering what it had been like to have that sort of enthusiasm. Yes, there was only five years between them, but college had pulled Emily away from what had once been a genuine interest and passion and shoved her into something that was supposed to evolve into a career. In that regard, five years felt like a lot.

Emily and Steve followed her to the front. Emily looked up into the dark glass of the bridge's windshield and saw Cliff looking to the depth finder and then to the water—then again and again, like one of those little plastic birds people put on their dashboards. He slid one of the windows open and his face was alight, like a kid looking under the tree at Christmas.

"It's close, guys," he hollered. "Any second now! Any s—"

Emily turned when he started yelling to them, just in time to see a massive shape rising towards the surface of the water roughly fifty yards ahead of them. Watching the shape of the whale grow closer and larger made her both elated and slightly nervous. This thing was big; if it was another thirty of forty yards closer, it could potentially cause some damage to the boat.

Then there was a rushing sound of water as its body broke the surface. Emily saw its grey hide, its long body and—

Suddenly, the silence that fell over the boat was not one of awe. It was the sort of silence that often came with bad news. It was heavy and unexpected.

What was breaking the surface of the water was not a blue whale. Instead, it was a shark. Only, that couldn't be right because sharks didn't grow to be this big. This was a shark the size of a blue whale—hell, probably even bigger than a blue whale. And that sort of thing just didn't exist.

It made a slight turn of its body, almost making a U-shape as the upper half of its body came out of the water and then fell back in. As it dove back into the water, Emily caught just the briefest glimpse if its mouth. Even only barely opened, it was cavernous.

She took a step back, a sound rising up in her throat. She was finally able to give that noise a shape and formed a word with it. "Cliff...?"

"What the hell was that?" Zoe asked.

"Looked like a shark," Cliff said. "But there's no way in hell a shark could grow to that size."

As that comment fell on their ears, the boat rocked slightly from the wake the splash of the thing has caused. Emily couldn't take her eyes off of the sea, afraid the thing would breach again, closer to the boat this time.

Steve spoke up from beside her. His voice was tinged with fear. She didn't think much of Steve but she had to admit—she had never seen or heard him in a state of fear. Hearing it now made the entire situation somehow worse.

"Where'd it go?" Steve asked.

Emily heard the slight movements of Cliff moving around in the bridge over their heads. She pictured him checking the depth finder and looking quickly back out to the water. After a few moments, he responded with relief in his voice.

"It's heading back down below," he called back. "And it's moving fast."

"Good," Zoe said. "But still...what the hell was it?"

Emily turned her head away from the water now, looking up to Cliff and hoping he had a satisfactory answer. But the fear and almost boy-like awe in his eyes did nothing but make her more nervous than before.

"It was a shark," he said. "I saw it, you saw it, we all saw it. It was without a doubt the biggest one I've ever seen, but it was a shark."

"That's impossible," Emily said, looking hopelessly up at him. "That thing was bigger than any *whale* I've ever seen, let alone a shark."

"Yeah," Steve said, "but how many whales have you actually seen?"

It was a good point, but it still infuriated her. She didn't bother with a response because it was embarrassing to admit that she had never seen one—only on television and in magazines.

"Don't be a smartass," Cliff said. "And besides…she's right. There's no shark I've ever seen or even heard of that is that big. And that's why you'd smell the faint scent of urine emanating from me if you were to come up to the bridge right now. That thing was a monster. It was a—"

He stopped here, his eyes quickly glancing away from his crew of three below and back to the depth finder and his other instrumentation in the bridge.

"What is it?" Emily asked.

"It's coming back up," Cliff said. It sounded like someone had punched him in the throat.

"What?" Zoe bellowed.

"What?" Steve said, his voice near panic now.

"Shit," Cliff said. His voice was shaky and breaking. "It's coming back up and it's going to be close. Hold on to something!"

There was a terrifying moment when Emily didn't think her legs were going to work. The idea of a shark of that size was impossible and made her think of nightmares she had on occasion where she was stranded at sea, knowing there was some monstrous leviathan waiting in the depths below her. Oddly, that dream had spurred her dreams of a possible career involving the ocean. She wanted to understand the depths and the enormity of it all.

She felt like she was asleep right then, waiting to be stirred awake as the fear reached its peak.

But no...the only thing that snapped her out of it was Zoe brushing by her to hold on to a metal pole that ran along the length of the central cabin. Steve was looking at her and she could see that he was torn between running for whatever cover there might be or to stay with her to see if she was okay. She nearly felt something for him in that moment. Maybe there *was* something more than some obsessive crush he had for her. If he was willing to stand by her in the midst of this and put himself in harm's way for her, what did that say about him?

She never got the chance to find out, though. Her legs decided to work and she followed Zoe, holding on to the metal bar. It was a lame plan, but the alternative was going inside and cowering and that seemed one thousand times worse.

The boat fell into dead silence and it allowed Emily to hear it. The damned thing was moving so fast to the surface that she could hear it moving through the water even before it breached.

And then it broke the surface in an explosion of water. The entire front of the boat was covered in water as the shark breached less than ten feet away from the left side of the boat. Emily screamed but it was drowned out by Zoe's shout of terror, as well as the thunderous noise the water made as it struck the boat. Through the water, Emily could see just enough of the shark to tell that it was arcing in its jump, aiming towards them.

It was going to hit them—just barely, but that would be more than enough to do some serious damage. Still screaming, the water cascading down around them in buckets so forceful that it was hard enough to push her back, the shark came down. When it did, she saw its face and truly understood its true size. It was at least three times as large as Cliff's rented boat and just the portion of its head that she could see through the torrent of water was going to likely be enough to destroy the boat.

When it hit the side of *The Gull*, the entire vessel surged hard to the right. Emily felt it tilt just as the cracking sounds filled the world. Something under her feet trembled and she nearly lost her footing. Beside her, Zoe was slipping as the boat teetered to the right. Emily knew the tilt wasn't nearly strong enough to tip them, but the sounds of destruction from the right were getting worse.

She dared a glance and saw that while the shark had not managed to sink its massive jaws into the boat, it had done enough damage by simply throwing its weight into it.

The rails up front were gone and the floor on which she now stood was splintered and jagged. She could see one of the cabins below through the hole in the floor. It was quickly filling with sea water.

"Get your asses up here *now!*" Cliff demanded from his perch in the bridge.

Emily turned to do just that and nearly collided with Steve. He was soaked and looked horrified but his attention was solely on her for the moment.

"Are you okay?" he asked her.

"Yeah."

He took her hand and there was nothing possessive about it. It felt safe and Emily didn't bother to dwell on that. Together, they ran to the right, fighting the tilt of the boat and the surge of water that had made the deck slippery. Along the starboard side, they found Zoe already heading for the cabin entrance, leaning against the wall of the cabin's exterior to keep from sliding.

They slipped a bit as they made their way to the cabin entrance. Inside, most everything had been thrown to the floor; the shelves were knocked loose, depositing food and electronics in piles at their feet. Something down below by their living quarters was making a dim sort of alarm noise but it was drowned out by the cabin taking on water.

They raced up the stairs to the bridge, again having to fight against the tilt of the boat. Emily hoped it was her imagination, but she thought it had gotten worse in the fifteen seconds or so it had taken them to move from the front of the boat to the stairs leading to the bridge.

In the bridge, Cliff seemed to be doing several things at once. He was holding the receiver to the CB radio and fiddling with the controls with one hand. With his other hand, he seemed to be attempting to make corrections to a piece of instrumentation that Emily had never seen before. All she knew was that everything up here was in disarray and nothing looked promising. She also saw that Cliff's eyes kept darting back to the depth finder and he looked very pale.

"How screwed are we?" Zoe asked.

"Royally," Cliff said, on the verge of tears. "I can't hear a damned thing on the radio. I've sent out a distress signal but at the rate we're taking on water, it won't matter. The boat will go under in less than fifteen minutes."

"What can we do?" Steve asked.

"There's a life raft under one of the benches in the central room below. But given what just tore a hole in this boat, I don't really care much for that idea. But it might be the only option we have available to us."

"So what do we—" Emily said, but was interrupted.

"It's coming back again," Cliff said, his eyes once again on the depth finder. Looking at the screen, he dropped the radio's receiver. It dangled from its cord like some poor beheaded animal.

"Where?" Steve asked.

"Dead ahead," Cliff said, pointing to the depth finder with a trembling finger. "And it's not coming up this time…now it's coming straight ahead, like a torpedo."

They huddled nervously around the depth finder. Emily felt herself wanting to cry but wouldn't allow it. She was already starting to shake and, she was surprised to find, still holding Steve's hand. More than that, she was gripping it tightly for some sort of reassurance.

"How far away is it?" Zoe asked.

"About a hundred meters and closing fast," Cliff said. "It must have swam back a few hundred feet just to pick up speed."

"Is there anything we can do?" Steve asked.

Cliff shook his head and there was a new sense of calm on his face. Emily thought it was a meager sort of acceptance. Still, he tried the radio again, pressing the receiver.

"Anyone out there, come in! We're being attacked by a shark…a big shark and…we need help. Our position is—"

He was interrupted by a massive creaking sound and then a popping noise that, to Emily, sounded like a tree being snapped in half. The boat seemed to buckle and the tilt increased by about ten degrees.

"Was that it?" Emily asked. "Did it just hit us?"

"No," Cliff said. He pointed to the depth finder and said, "It's still forty meters out. That was just the boat. We're taking on water very fast. If this thing doesn't tear the boat apart, we'll have water coming up the stairs in less than five minutes." He paused here, gulped while looking at the depth finder, and said: "Twenty meters."

"What the hell do we *do?*" Steve asked.

"Hold tight and pray."

"I don't pray," Zoe said.

"Learn," Cliff said. "Ten meters, eight…"

Emily looked to the front of the boat and saw the shape of it through the glass. It was still underwater, but barely. Its fin had breached and tore through the water like a knife. And God help them, it looked nearly as big as the boat. It was coming at them just like Cliff had said: like a torpedo, tearing through the water.

She let out a moan and then the world seemed to fall away all around her. The boat was shaken violently, followed by an enormous explosion of wood and glass. She felt herself being thrown backwards, her grip on Steve's hand released as she slammed into something hard. She could make no sense of anything; she tumbled and struck hard objects at every turn. Something soft and wet hit her in the head and she was pretty sure she felt someone's hand brush against her arm. Then all of that was gone and she felt herself falling. She barely saw the entire front of the bridge—glass, walls, and Cliff's instrumentation panel—come crashing forward before she felt herself falling backwards into impossible emptiness.

It's the stairs to the main area, she thought. *I'm falling down the stairs and—*

Then there was water everywhere and something hard struck her leg. She tried to cry out but when she did, warm salt water filled her mouth. She lashed out with her arms and legs, panicking rather than swimming, taking a while to understand that somehow, in less than five seconds, she had gone from standing in the bridge, to being underwater.

Something massive passed by her on the left. She didn't see it in the commotion of wood, debris, and water, but the force of its passing spun her like a top. It took that brush with the thing that had destroyed the boat to snap her out of her frantic state. She went still for a moment and looked at the destruction all around her. Bits of wood were everywhere, as were random poles, pipes and other assorted debris. Salt water stung her eyes. It was all very murky but she could still make out most of her surroundings.

Above her, she saw a leg kicking for the surface and that seemed like a marvelous idea. She did the same just as she started to feel her chest tightening from lack of air. She swam for the surface, already certain that it would do nothing more than delay the inevitable.

Somewhere out there, that monstrosity was surely looping back around to gulp down the morsels that it had just knocked out of the boat.

7

She came up to the surface, took in a huge gulp of air, and used it to scream. The boat has been reduced to a few large chunks of material and smaller splintered fragments. To her right, bobbing in the wake of the enormous shark, she could see what appeared to be the starboard side of the boat, rapidly sinking. Somewhere behind her, she heard Zoe screaming.

Emily turned in that direction, treading water that was littered with the ruins of a boat that had been mostly whole less than a minute ago. She saw Zoe clambering on top of a chunk of the boat's siding roughly the size of a twin bed. Emily looked frantically around but saw no sign of Cliff or Steve.

She then cast her eyes a little further out beyond the wreckage and debris. She recalled seeing that massive fin breaking the water; if she saw it now, she felt that she might very well freeze in fear. She'd drown or let the thing devour her. Maybe it would be over quick. Drowning couldn't really be *that* bad, could it?

As she searched for that imminent sign of death, she saw another person come up from underwater, gasping for breath. It was Cliff, roughly twenty feet away from her. He had surfaced near what looked like a steel drum from the boat's inner workings. The right side of his face was covered in blood and his eyes were drawn wide open. He looked like a madman as he swam furiously towards her.

Seeing him move with such purpose finally unlocked whatever primal need was buried within her as well. She turned and started swimming for the same plank Zoe was now resting on. Seeing that Emily was headed her way, Zoe leaned forward a bit and extended her hand. Emily swam as fast as she could, waiting for a razor-like sensation to envelop her at any moment as the shark tore into her. *To hell with that,* she thought. *I saw the mouth on that thing. If it wanted, it could just swallow me whole and not even get its teeth dirty in the process. It would be like swallowing a pill. I'd still be alive when it swallowed me.*

This made her swim faster and she was reaching for Zoe's hand within a few seconds. They worked together quickly, easily pulling Emily up onto the plank. Now that she was on it, Emily saw that it was a large portion of the main deck—the same deck they had been standing on when Cliff had first pointed out the location of what he thought was a sperm whale.

Zoe was shuddering beside her, and Emily could relate. While she was not visibly shaking, she felt *something* taking place inside of her. Her heart was thrumming and her head felt swimmy. She also felt like she might puke at any given moment.

She looked back out to Cliff from her unsteady perch. He was swimming slowly now. His head seemed to be spouting blood and he looked to be favoring his right shoulder. She saw his blood gushing out into the water and knew that it was bad news. They might as well have set out a welcome mat for the shark.

She looked around for anything to push in Cliff's direction although she knew it would be useless; the water was too tumultuous to float anything over to him.

As she looked around, she saw the hull along the back of the boat where the engine was located. It bobbed up and down almost comically about ten feet away from her. She nearly looked right past it but then saw Steve. He was sitting inside of it, pushed almost against the engine and looking out like a scared child from under their covers at night.

Feeling a bit of relief rise up inside of her because they had all managed to survive, Emily looked back out to Cliff.

Her sense of relief was immediately obliterated.

Coming up fast beside him was a massive shape rising out of the water. By the time her eyes had properly seen it, the top half of the shark's head surfaced, its massive jaws springing open.

Cliff started to scream. It was a high-pitched shout that barely broke over the roar of the ocean before it abruptly stopped. Emily watched it happen in a frozen state of fear from her place on the plank. There was nothing violent or bloody about it at all. Cliff was simply there one minute and gone the next. Although the large mouth of the shark fully encompassed Cliff's floating body, it was so large that it didn't so much as dirty its teeth when it closed its jaws over him and swallowed him whole.

Zoe had seen this happen, too. Emily felt the younger girl next to her. She was shuddering and drawing in deep breaths. Seeing the stark terror on Zoe's face triggered something in Emily. She felt her nerves loosen and her brain was firing on all synapses all of a sudden.

No, she had never seen a shark up close before but she knew a great deal about them. She tried to draw up all of that knowledge and focus on it…not only to keep her mind from letting the fear in, but also in the hopes of keeping the rest of them alive.

She slowly reached over, careful not to cause their plank to tilt one way or the other, and slowly placed a hand on Zoe's shoulder. In that touch, Emily could feel a great tension as something started to build inside of her. A scream, Emily thought.

"Zoe," she whispered. "You have to stay quiet. Maybe it'll leave. But if you scream right now, it's going to hear it and it's going to come back."

Zoe nodded and started biting at her lip, as if to keep the scream locked inside. Emily assumed that Steve likely wouldn't be able to put this together for himself, so she looked back in his direction. He remained cowering in the bobbing section of the boat that held the engine. His eyes were locked on her when she gave him the *shhh* gesture of a single finger to her lips. He nodded, his eyes like those of a scared animal hiding in a burrow. She again saw something fragile in his stare and she was confused to find that she wanted him to be by her side.

Feeling Zoe's tremors pass through her arm, Emily looked back around at the waters. She dreaded the idea of seeing that monstrous dorsal fin break the surface of the water. Her heart quaked every time she saw a piece of debris from the boat that her mind instantly thought was a fin.

There was an eerie silence to the sea. Emily could picture the remains of *The Gull* sinking to the bottom where it would lay for an extended amount of time before it was later discovered as nothing more than a sad setting to a story of death that no one would ever fully know.

"Emily?" Zoe whispered.

"Yeah?"

"What the hell are we supposed to do now?" The girl was still shuddering with shock and the physical effort of keeping her grief in. Emily gave the girl a cursory examination and could see no visible injuries. They at least had *that* going for them.

"I don't know," Emily said.

That was an understatement. She had only a rough idea of where they were located so she didn't know how close the nearest possibility of help might be. More than that, she was not the best swimmer. She looked to the sky and saw that it was getting dark. Nightfall was still a few hours off, but the gathering storm clouds in the north made the idea of being out here in the dark a bit more ominous.

She then looked out to the sea, her heart sagging. In her twenty-three years of life, she had never quite decided if she believed in God or not. Still, she found herself hoping as she floated on that plank—hoping that there *was* a God and that He was still in the business of handing out miracles.

8

About forty minutes passed before any of them dared to say anything. Emily had spent those forty minutes with the certainty that the shark was somewhere directly beneath them—that it would surface at any moment and swallow them whole, just as it had done with Cliff. She had busied herself with trying to get a gauge on their situation, right down to the most minute of details.

For instance, to her left, floating a bit behind the hull that Steve still hid in, she had spotted one of the built-in benches from the front of the ship. She recalled watching Cliff dig through one of them, checking for supplies before they'd pulled away from the coast.

About half of the bench was sticking out of the water, the lower part submerged. As they floated in the water, the bench was closing in on them very slowly. It inched its way towards Steve, like it was sneaking up on him. Emily wondered what might be inside of it. Really, there was nothing much that could help them in this situation. Even if there was an inflatable life raft in there, it would mean nothing if the shark came back. The same was true of water or food. All that would accomplish was giving them full stomachs when they were eaten.

"Emily?"

Zoe's voice from beside her made her jump. She sounded like a frightened ten-year-old girl, hoping that anyone might be able to provide some comfort.

"What?"

"That shark," she said. "It was just *too* big. Sharks don't get that big."

"I don't know," Emily said. "I've read stories about some massive great whites."

"Not *that* massive," Zoe said. "The size of that thing…"

She trailed off for a moment and Emily watched as something dawned in her eyes. She had made a connection of some sort and it had terrified her.

"What is it?" Emily asked.

"You've heard of the megalodon, right?"

Emily wanted to roll her eyes and dismiss the idea. Yes, she had heard of megalodons. They were sharks that were believed to have thrived in prehistoric times, during the Cenozoic Era. They were thought to have once been a ferocious predator with no equal. But evidence suggested that they had died out shortly after dinosaurs went instinct. The megalodon had been a massive shark, a beast that seemed tailor made for hunting. The most unbelievable aspect of the creature was that it was believed to have grown to lengths as long as sixty feet.

And while Emily firmly stood in the camp that doubted the megalodon had survived whatever cataclysmic event had wiped out its prehistoric brethren, the last hour of her life had her switching camps. Still, it was hard to fathom that a legendary megalodon had torn their boat to shreds.

The size *did* match up, though. And there was no mistaking it—they had been attacked by a shark. Emily had seen its face and torso quite clearly as it had breached that first time.

"Yes," she said, trying to derail her train of thought from where it was unmistakably heading. "But I think that's a long shot."

"Do you really?" Zoe asked, clearly picking up on the hesitation in her voice.

"I don't know," Emily admitted. While the idea itself seemed sort of preposterous, it was also the only thing that made any real sense. She also knew that she wanted Zoe to shut the hell up before her whispers became a normal voice. As far as Emily was concerned, even whispering was too loud.

She looked back out to Steve again and saw that he had managed to stretch out a bit more. She wondered if he might be smarter than she thought. He had positioned himself inside the hull so that he was not only free from most of the restrictions that the engine took up, but the chunk of boat also seemed to be tottering a little more evenly in the water.

He caught her looking at him and waved. She waved back, looking beyond the hull to where the fragmented bench floated. It was getting closer to him, but achingly slow. There were probably twenty feet or so between Steve and that bench. And besides, who was to say there was anything that could help them inside of it.

She looked to the sky again, this time hoping for a random passing helicopter rather than an attentive god. But the sky was just as blank as ever. Looking there, she also thought about airplanes and how there could be hundreds of people flying overhead, unaware of the deadly situation a twenty-three-year-old grad student was in thousands of feet below them. She then thought of little plastic cups of soda and the ability to watch a movie on the back of the seat in front of you. She had no idea why, but she suddenly found that thought achingly funny.

Is this what it feels like to go delirious?

Maybe. But she wasn't going to allow herself the experience.

She then thought of her mom, whom had likely just gotten off of such a plane in San Diego. She had flown out to see her other daughter—the daughter that had landed a safe office job straight out of college where she was some sort of assistant to a finance lawyer.

Of course, Emily had scoffed at that. Why sit in an office when you could set out and see the world? And if you could help save a species or two in the process, all the better, right?

She again felt a panicked sort of laugh creeping up her throat. She seriously began to wonder if she was having some sort of weird panic attack out in the Pacific Ocean, at least twenty miles away from the nearest land. She looked out to the water, wondering how much time had passed. She had a watch but never wore it. It was now probably at the bottom of the ocean with the rest of the things in her bag. She glanced over to Zoe and saw that she wore a Fitbit on her left arm. The time on it read 5:48.

That meant they'd been out here, floating around on the remains of a destroyed boat, for a little over an hour and a half.

"Hey…"

The voice broke her from her daze. It was Steve's voice, whispered and sounding hopeful.

"What?" Emily said, annoyed. Did neither of these morons know what it meant to remain quiet?

"Do you think it's gone?" he asked.

"I don't know." The truth was, she thought it probably had. But even if it was a good distance away and they started yelling for help, the commotion would do nothing more than draw the damned thing back to them.

"Well, what can we do?" he whispered. "We can't just sit here and hope another boat comes by."

She shrugged, although she was thinking: *That might be our only option.* Still, wanting to do what she could to inject some hope into their horrifying predicament, she looked back to the bench.

"There's a bench floating around behind you," she whispered. "It's one of the benches Cliff was putting stuff in when we were loading up. It's coming towards you, but it's a good ways back. It will take some time, but it'll get there."

"What's in it?" Steve asked.

"No idea," Emily said.

"There might be an emergency radio or something," Zoe said from beside her. Emily was pretty sure that there had been no such a thing on *The Gull* and even if there was, why the hell would it be in a basic storage bench?

"Maybe," she said, figuring a little hope might do them all some good.

"So we just wait, then?" Steve asked.

"I guess so."

He gave her a look that indicated he wasn't pleased with this answer, but he said nothing else. He looked out to the water beyond them, seemed to think about something, and then looked away.

"Someone will come, right?" Zoe asked her. Sitting beside one another, she was able to barely whisper and still be heard over the lush and hypnotic noises of the ocean.

"I'd think so," she said. "Cliff's friend on the radio knows he was out here. I imagine he'd try getting in touch with him again. There's also the rental place…they'll be looking for us to bring the boat back tomorrow night."

"That's another whole day out here," Zoe said. "Not to mention a full night."

"Yeah," Emily said. "Just trying to be realistic."

"Well, being realistic sucks." A tear slipped out of her eye and it nearly made Emily cry as well. The mere thought of floating around out here for another day or so was unbearable and made her feel sick.

"It does," Emily admitted.

They fell into silence again. Thunder rumbled somewhere very far off and Emily looked back to the rain clouds to the north. They were darker now, making the approaching dusk seem a little more threatening than it should. The clouds were getting closer and she supposed they'd have rain to contend with soon, as if things weren't already bad enough.

At some point, Zoe started to cry. They were small, shuddering little gasps as she continued to try to keep the bulk of the noise in. Emily, feeling incredibly awkward, placed an arm around her shoulders. She barely knew the girl—an awkward few conversations during Zoe's College for a Weekend excursion hardly founded a friendship—and had no opinion of her one way or the other. She was a little *too* driven and, Emily thought, was going to be the kind of woman that likely never married because she wouldn't have time for the attention and needs of a husband. It was a shame, too; she was incredibly pretty.

The sky darkened slowly and Emily was amazed to find that she had slipped into some sort of fugue state. Perhaps it was the trauma of the situation, or the movement of the waves lulling her into a form of hypnosis—whatever it was, the next time she looked to Zoe's Fitbit, it was 7:06.

She looked over to Steve and saw that he was looking up into the darkened hull, observing the slight concave space over his head. She looked to the right of the hull and saw that the bench was now remarkably close to the hull. It wasn't yet within an arm's reach, but it was close.

"Steve," she said, her voice a hissed whisper.

His head jerked a bit, as if he had been dozing, and he looked at her, eager to speak to her. "Yeah?"

"The bench," she said. "It's coming up on your right."

Steve moved around a bit, awkwardly getting out of the half-sitting state he had been in for the last few hours, and then managed to get on his knees. He seemed to think about something for a while and then nodded, as if agreeing with himself.

"What are you doing?" she asked.

"If I put my weight to the left side, this thing tilts. Too much weight on that side and I think I'd sink. But with my weight on that side, I can also sort of turn this thing a little."

Stupid, she thought, directing it towards herself. *You never even stopped to think about how he'd actually open the bench, did you? He'd almost* have *to get out into the water.*

But she knew how Steve was thinking. In the water or in his little hull….what did it matter? Floating around on the wreckage of a boat was the same as being the water when you were talking about a beast the size of the one they were dealing with.

"Be careful," she whispered.

He smiled at her and, God help him, he looked delighted with himself. She watched as he shifted most of his weight to the left. As he had said, the hull tilted that way, bobbing a bit before starting to fully commit to the total shift. As it started to tilt, Steve put his arm in the water and gave a few furious paddling motions. With each one, Emily couldn't help but cringe.

As she watched him manage to turn the section of the destroyed engine hull, everything seemed to work perfectly. It turned just enough so that he could see the bench approaching. When he was able to see it, the bench *had* come to within arm's reach. He reached out and pulled it towards him. As he did, the hull shifted a bit more and more of it went under water. Somewhere along its broken base, it was starting to take on water.

Emily and Zoe watched as Steve opened the seat compartment of the bench. When he did, he had to lean out of the hull to keep the bench from tottering over backward and spilling its contents out into the water. In doing so, he nearly fell into the water himself.

Through the darkening dusk, Emily saw a smile on his face.

"What is it?" she asked.

Steve reached in and pulled out something. He looked at it, testing it in his hands, before showing it to them.

A flare gun.

"Not too bad," he said. "Only, there's nothing else we can really use in here. Lifejackets, some twine, a bunch of empty boxes and a manual for the engine."

"You know how to work that?" Emily asked, pointing to the flare gun.

"No. But it can't be hard, right?"

Emily watched him observe it as well as he could in the gloom of dusk. Actually, the dusk had nearly managed to become night. She looked up into the sky and saw that the rainclouds were close now. She felt certain that if the sound of the lapping sea weren't in her ears, she'd be able to hear rainfall nearby.

"Okay," he said after thirty seconds or so. "I think I got it figured out. Is there any certain direction to shoot it?"

"Up," Zoe said.

Ignoring Zoe's sarcastic and panic-laced comment, Emily thought about it for a moment. "Probably to the east," she said. "I figure more boats will be closer to land that further out to sea." She had no idea if this was right or not, but she *had* to have some sort of plan to keep herself from freaking out.

"Okay," Steve said.

"Before you get trigger happy," Emily said, "why not throw us two life jackets? If we end up back in the water for some reason—"

"Don't even go there," Zoe said, cutting her off. "But yeah…lifejackets would be nice."

Steve momentarily placed the flare gun back in the bench while he carefully pulled out the jackets. He tossed them underhanded towards the plank and Emily was able to catch both of them. However, putting it on without rocking the plank she and Zoe were sitting on was easier said than done.

While they worked together to get their lifejackets on, Steve also buckled his up. He then reached back into the bench for the flare gun. He peered to the direction they had agreed upon and Emily could see him gathering his courage. She wondered if he knew that a good deal of their chances of being rescued soon were literally in his hands.

She saw that he had to lean out of the hull to get a good angle for the shot. He used the top of the broken bench to steady himself and that seemed to do the trick. He took a moment to raise his arm, his body shaking on the unsteady footing of the wobbling hull. He winced as he pulled the trigger and the sound of it startled him. He nearly fell into the water with the gun still in his hand.

The gun made a hissing sound that reminded Emily of her white noise maker back at home. A split second later, a flare erupted from it. A red arc of light shot upwards and slightly to the east. The three of them watched it go, an uneventful little firework in the gathering night.

As it streaked across the sky, Emily felt the first drops of rain on her face.

Then, to her left, there was a quick *"Shit!"*

This was followed by a splashing noise as Steven lost his footing and fell into the water.

9

The last of the six rovers was being securely buckled along the back of the MarineEx boat when Carl spotted the thin trail of red light in the sky to the northeast of them. He knew it for what it was the moment he saw it. The flare hadn't been shot from extremely close by, but it hadn't been that far away, either.

He watched it complete its arc as he fastened the last clasp on the latch. The vacuum system made its tell-tale shutdown noises ten minutes ago and with the ROVs and the Collector fastened down, the day was essentially over. The vacuum was being emptied by the shutdown blowers, a series of simple air jets spaced throughout the pump to ensure bits of detritus and debris weren't left in the system to create clogs the next time the system was in use.

He was latching the ROVs down because Trevor has basically reported that he was done working for the day the moment he had instructed the ROVs and the Collector to come to the surface.

Carl didn't mind. He'd gladly do this grunt work to keep Trevor's mouth shut. Besides...for the moment, he wasn't concerned with Trevor and his irritable moods. He was more concerned with that red flare.

"Hey, Bo!" he called out.

He gave Bo a few seconds, knowing that he'd be up in the main cabin with Trevor. Trevor, though, would be starting at the instrument panel, ensuring that the pump and filtration system were shutting down property. So, as usual, Trevor would be of no use.

Bo showed up about thirty seconds later, coming out of the cabin and out onto the deck. "You called me?"

"I did. Did either of you see a flare from inside?"

"A flare? No. I was going over the last string of readings from the day."

"I figured," Carl said. "But right over there," he said, pointing to where he had seen the flare arc and then fizzle out as it had dropped towards the ocean, "I saw a flare. It died out about thirty seconds ago."

"A vessel in distress, you think?" Bo asked.

"I don't know. But flares at sea…never really a good thing."

"Want me start the engines and head over there?"

"Yeah. We might as well have a look."

"Will do."

Bo headed back into the cabin, leaving Carl alone again. He looked towards the place where the flare had originated from. It was cloaked in dark and out of his sight. He hated the fact that the dead whale from earlier in the day popped into his mind as he peered out into that darkness. But it was there, torn open and dead despite its size and majestic nature.

He felt and heard the boat's engine come to life less than a minute later. As they started moving, he headed into the cabin. Everything had been shut down by the time he got there and Trevor did not seem happy. He'd wanted to run thing for another hour or so but Carl had been instructed by MarineEx to not run the ROVs after dusk. It had something to do with the ability of the sensors to detect the direction the ROVs were headed as they were brought to the surface. It was yet another thing that went over Carl's head.

Up in the bridge, Trevor was in his corner, his face awash in the greed and red glow of his system's panels and computer screens. Bo was behind the wheel. While he wasn't much of a sailor, he did know his way around the bridge and was the only other person Carl had ever worked with at MarineEx that he'd allow behind the wheel of one of his boats.

"So we got a flare, did we?" Trevor asked, not bothering to look up from his readings and analytics.

"Yeah."

"We going to play hero, I take it?"

"No," Carl said. "We're just going to do the right thing. I don't think it came from too far away. It won't hurt to check it out."

Trevor made a grunt of response, his head still lowered like a monk as he looked over his screens. Carl thought about getting on the radio to call the flare in to the proper authorities but decided against it. He'd hold off on such measures until they actually saw something out at sea. For all he knew, the flare could have been the result of pranksters. He'd heard stories of such things and didn't want to have to put up with Trevor's snide remarks afterwards. Also, there was the fact that much of the equipment on their boat was classified.

He walked over to Bo and gave him a clap on the shoulder. "I'll take it from here," he said. "Thanks."

Bo nodded, stepping away from the helm and giving it up to Carl. For a moment, both men looked out into the dark waters, the night pressing down on the sea like a heavy quilt. Carl flipped a switch to the right of the wheel and a pair of lights along the front of the boat came on. Their glow wasn't very strong, illuminating the water only about twenty yards or so ahead of them.

"Bo, do you mind heading up top to keep an eye out to the left and right?" Carl asked.

"Sure thing," Bo said. He seemed excited to be a part of something that could be potentially exciting. Trevor, meanwhile, might as well have been off in some other boat, floating along by himself.

Carl steered ahead, listening to Bo's soft footfalls as he walked up the stairwell and to the look-out deck overhead. As he navigated forward, Carl was struck with the harrowing concept of being stranded at sea. It had crossed his mind before, particularly six years ago when one of MarineEx's very first experimental vessels had stalled out and been unresponsive for five hours one hundred miles out into the Atlantic. He'd been on that boat and it was a journey that came back to haunt him every now and then.

At night, though…that was something altogether. The depth of the water was bad enough, but when you threw in dark skies and a shadowed horizon where anything at all could be waiting in the water…just thinking of that gave him the creeps.

He pushed the boat a little harder, still well within the engine's much-tested limits. Trevor gave him a brief glance of annoyance and then returned his attention to the day's readings and data.

He glared at the night-veiled sea ahead, keeping his eyes open for any sign of someone in distress. He started to notice a light rain falling, just enough to become annoying on the windshield of the cabin. After he'd been on course for roughly ten miles, he started to wonder about just giving it up. Tomorrow was going to be a long day—longer still if they got no real results, as Trevor would start to pout about not having enough time again.

Before he could give the idea of calling it quits any real thought, he heard Bo's voice. It was getting closer with each word, punctuated by footfalls approaching down the stairs.

"Signs of wreckage to the east," Bo said. "Take a gentle right and we'll be headed straight for it."

Carl felt his heart start to beat a little faster. He also noticed that now that there was a clear sign of some sort of trouble. Trevor's interest was now peaked.

"A boat?" Carl asked.

"I'd safely say so," Bo said. He came back behind the helm again, looking out through the widow and to the night outside.

As far as Carl was concerned, the water seemed even more menacing just due to the fact that Bo had confirmed the wreckage. This was heightened when he saw the first bits for himself. A splintered section of wood, about two feet long and six feet wide bobbed in the water, eerie-looking in the lights atop the boat. Some sort of cloth rode small waves directly behind it.

Carl put the engine into neutral as they coasted closer to the debris. It didn't take him long to see the worst of it. The ocean softly bounced their boat, making the small flood lights go up and down, revealing the scene a bit further out only to have the lights then fall back several yards.

In the crest of one of the small waves, Carl caught sight of something that nearly made him shout in surprise.

Two women were huddled together on a plank of splintered wood. They were soaked—from the ocean or the rain was anyone's guess—and looked, for just a moment, like ghosts in the boat lights.

"Oh my God," he said, instantly heading for the stairs. He nearly fell down them as he called back behind him. "Bo, bring he boat in a little closer. Let's get them on board!"

Carl reached the stern and found that the rain was surprisingly cold and coming down a bit harder than he had thought. He ran to the side of the boat and saw the women clearly just as Bo started the engine. Looking out, Carl also saw a third person with them. It was a man, half-on and half-off of what looked to be a ship's engine compartment.

"Thank God!" one of the women shouted. She was small with black hair and looked incredibly pale in the glow of the flood lights.

"I see three out there," Carl called out to them. "Are there any more of you?"

"No," the other girl said. "There were four of us, but one of them is…he's dead."

The boat puttered closer and Trevor was suddenly standing beside him with life vests in his hands. There also a life preserver—one of the hard circular ones—around his forearm. *When did he suddenly decide to be useful?* Carl wondered.

"Well, let's get you guys in," Carl said, shielding his face from the rain.

"Thank you so much!" the girl closest to him said.

"Are you good with the life jackets you have on?" he asked. "We have more if you need them?"

"No, we're good."

"Are you injured? Can you swim to the back of our boat? There's a ladder back here."

"No one is injured," said the girl with black hair. "But there's...there's no way I'm getting in the water."

"It'll be okay," Carl said. "Let's just take it one step at a time and—"

"No. I'm not getting in the water."

"What's your name?" Carl asked, trying to get her mind over the fear of the water.

"Zoe."

"Well, Zoe...there's less than fifteen feet between us now. By the time you get off that plank, it'll be less than that. I think you can manage. We'll get as close as we can, okay?"

"Okay," she said with some reservation.

With that, Trevor raced to the back of the boat, skidding along around the ROVs and heading for the ladder. He unfastened the latch, letting down their metal ladder, which stretched out to a depth of three feet...

"What the hell do you think happened to them?" Trevor quietly asked.

"I have no idea," Carl whispered. "That boat...it's absolutely destroyed."

"Probably shouldn't ask them until they get on board," Trevor said. "It might slow them down...maybe freak them out."

"That's what I was thinking," Carl agreed. He was pleasantly surprised at how calm and logical Trevor seemed to be in a crisis. It almost made him not hate the man. *Almost.*

They stood along the rail until all three of them had their lifejackets on. When they started to swim for the boat, Carl ran to the back and let down the ladder. The engine was idling, leaving an almost non-existent wake.

The man had reached the women and seemed to stop to check on them. After a moment, the blonde woman that seemed to have her act together slowly slipped into the water. The one called Zoe let out a squeak of disapproval.

With the blonde woman and the man in the water, Zoe remained where she was. Carl could hear the other girl talking to her, trying to coax her in. After a while, Zoe nodded and slipped in.

It broke Carl's heart to her the way she cried when she was in the water. But there was little he could do other than watch them cover the right feet or so between their plank and the back of his boat.

He watched them come, Zoe taking up the back of their little line. Her cries drowned out the rain and the idling engine, carrying across the waters like the sirens of folklore.

Then the crying stopped and she screamed.

It was a scream that sent a bolt of fear straight through Carl; it was a scream of utter terror, of a woman who was looking death in the face.

Then everyone in the water was screaming and before Carl saw what they were screaming about, he heard a rushing of water as something big broke the surface. Carl saw what it was, but his brain didn't seem to make the leap on its own. It was too muddled with thoughts like: *it's too big to be a shark* and *no, that makes no sense.*

But then the terror gripped him, too. He managed to not scream and for that, he was thankful. But by the time he was able to move and take action, it was far too late.

10

When the megalodon broke the surface of the water, Emily could literally feel the water all around her being churned in a mad sort of frenzy. She could feel the force of the thing tearing through the water and for a minute, she feared she might get sucked under. It all happened so fast that it took her a moment to make sense of her location—right and left were mixed up, making her feel dizzy. The night was partly to blame, but it was mostly the fear that surged through her.

Finally, she was able to tell where the commotion was coming from. It was directly behind her. She chanced a look over her shoulder just in time to see the shark hit the water again, going back down. It had missed Zoe by less than a few feet. Still, the crashing waves left in its path were immense. Emily caught the briefest glimpse of Zoe being essentially erased by one of the waves as it shoved her forward towards the boat.

Steve was between them and his eyes were locked on the boat with an intense focus. As much as Emily hated to do it, she knew that she had to do the same. Yes, Zoe was in the rear of their line and she had almost been crushed by a prehistoric creature that should have been dead long ago…but she still needed to get her ass to the boat to make sure she made it out of this alive.

She was certain the thing would come back, and quick. Still, it was massive, and it would need to go deep in order to swing back around to come for them. She recalled the window of time that had passed between the original breach and the attack on Cliff's boat. She figured she had about twenty or thirty seconds.

Fortunately, the force of the megalodon's splash propelled her forward. Her hand was touching the metal surface of the ladder within a matter of seconds following the splash and she wasted no time trying to climb it. She made it only two rungs up before she felt a hand fall over her wrist. She looked up and saw the first man that had come out and spoken to them. He gave a hard tug, bringing her up the ladder and safely onto the back of the boat.

The relief of being out of the water and on something solid was fleeting when she realized that she could feel the violence of the shark's wake rocking against the boat. She sat up quickly and looked back out to the water. All she could see was that same man hunched over, now helping Steve up out of the water.

The second man that had been on the side of the boat—the one that had let the ladder down on the back of the boat—approached her and put a hand on her shoulder. "Come on," he said. "Let's get you inside, out of the rain."

She could hear the fear in his voice. He'd seen what had just come out of the water. She wondered if he'd had the time to do the math: that something so big had torn apart the boat these three strangers had been on and that it could likely do the same to *his* boat.

Emily nodded to him but neither of them moved. The man at the ladder had gotten Steve up and he was crawling over to her. Steve's eyes, like Emily's, were back out at sea, though. They both saw that the man at the back of the boat was no longer moving. He looked back to them and gave a defeated shrug.

"She won't come any further," he said, looking back out to the water.

Over the rain and water slapping at the back of the boat, Emily could just barely hear Zoe's shuddering noises. She wasn't speaking, but was making a choked sort of crying. She sounded like some trapped and wounded animal.

The man at the ladder looked back to them and said, "She's frozen."

From the way he said it, Emily knew that he really didn't care. His mind was elsewhere—namely on the huge beast that had just leaped out of the water.

Emily got to her feet and stumbled towards the rail along the back of the boat. She felt Steve reaching for her, but she jerked away. She looked out and saw Zoe in the water, bobbing aimlessly. Her eyes looked lifeless, but her head was moving. She was looking for any signs of the dorsal fin that had torn through their boat or the nightmarish face that had opened its jaws and swallowed Cliff whole.

Emily opened her mouth to speak but the first words were locked in her throat as she saw something rising up from the bottom of the ocean. She had no idea *how* she saw it; the lights on the boat offered very little and the rain clouds blocked out the moonlight. Still, she saw it and it made her knees unhinge. She dropped to her knees and was helpless but to watch.

She saw the head of the megalodon racing for the surface, no more than ten feet below them. Its mouth was already partially opened. Zoe was directly in the center of it and she seemed to grow smaller as the shark got closer. Just before it broke the surface, Emily looked into that dark maw, darker than the night-shrouded sea. It was an abyss in there—a dark hell of things unimagined. It was bottomless and there was no escaping it.

Zoe was able to let out a single cry before the megalodon breached, its mouth perfectly taking her in and swallowing her whole. It actually looked as if Zoe was falling into some deep, dark hole. Emily barely had time to see this, though. The bottom half of the shark's enormous jaw hit the bottom of the boat, lifting the back half of the vessel into the air. Something cracked and popped beneath Emily as her legs were thrown out from beneath her.

She screamed as she felt herself being pitched forward. She was rising up and then quickly coming back down as the boat dropped back towards the water. Her knees slid along the rain-slickened surface of the boat, taking her directly towards the water. She wasn't going to be able to catch herself and—

She felt a hand clamp around her wrist, keeping her from falling off. She looked back, her heart thumping in her throat it seemed, and saw Steve. He looked terrified but when his eyes found hers, she was surprised to find that it helped. God help her, she felt *safe* with him. This was the second time he'd saved her in the last four hours or so.

"Hold on!" came a man's voice from her right.

She looked and saw the man at the back of the ladder, looking out into the water. As the boat steadied itself back out in the frantic water, Emily looked over the rail and saw that the man that had let the ladder down for them had fallen off the back of the boat during the attack. He was swimming frantically for the ladder but was being tossed in the chaotic waves left behind by the megalodon.

Emily watched as the man beside her went to the rail and yanked off the circular life preserver that hung there. Emily watched as the man that had pulled her onto the boat tossed the ring out, the white rope attached to it unspooling through his hands.

She then realized that she and Steve were still sitting on the stern. She was leaning into him, watching in horror as events unfolded in front of them. They were both shuddering when she saw a third man come running onto the stern from the cabin. He looked Asian and was a relatively short man. He was holding a large walkie-talkie device in his hand but it hung limply by his side as he looked out to the water.

As Emily watched, this man's mouth hung open in a soundless scream. Almost afraid to do so, Emily followed his gaze. Before her eyes took in the sight, she heard Steve whispering just beside her.

"No...Oh God..."

But she looked out and saw it anyway. The megalodon was coming up again, almost lazily this time. The top of its massive head came up above the water and then submerged again, as if it was simply checking out the scene. Perhaps it was the odd lighting or the night itself, but the thing looked evil as it surfaced. The man in the water started to panic and came swimming for the boat in a series of over-exaggerated strokes. Emily knew that this was the absolute worst thing he could do, but she was unable to shout out to him.

"Trevor," the man at the rail said, "you have to stop! It will see your legs moving and come after—"

He was interrupted by a blood-curdling scream from the man in the water—Trevor, apparently.

Emily was certain she saw the man go about ten shades of pale in less than a second. His screams became infant-like wails as the most basic part of his brain took over, awash in dread. Before she could understand what had happened to him, the shark's head came up again from directly behind him. Its jaws opened quickly and when it closed down, its teeth punctured directly through the top of his head. The man died with a scream falling dead in his throat, his mouth stretched wide and his eyes filled with horror.

In a violent jerking motion, the man was rolled over and under in a spray of dark fluid that could only be blood. When his body was pulled under, he was upside down. Before his corpse was pulled under the water, Emily saw what she assumed had caused his initial bought of screaming. His left leg was missing, chewed off in a grisly stump almost all the way up to his waist.

The man with the rope from the life ring threw it into the water as if it were a poisonous snake. He then took a few ambling steps back, muttering a string of curses under his breath. When he collided with the Asian man, he let out a shriek.

They both turned to look at Emily and Steve. She could tell that they were hoping they could provide some answers. It made her feel sorry for them and no safer than she had been out on the plank in the water.

"Is that what took down your boat?" the Asian man asked.

"Yes," Emily said.

"I've never seen a shark that big," the other man said.

"I don't know that I've ever seen *anything* that big," the Asian man said.

Steve looked to the two men with the same sort of hope she'd seen in the strangers' eyes moments ago. "So what can we do?" Steve asked. "What can we do right now to make sure it doesn't destroy *this* boat, too?"

"We're going to get the hell out of here," the man that seemed to be in charge said. "And we're going to send out a distress call.

Bo," he said, turning to the Asian man, "can you put the call in? I'll get our guests inside and situated."

"Sure," Bo said. "But what do I tell them?"

"That we've got survivors of a shark attack and at least two people are dead."

"And…well, what can we do if it comes back for more?" Bo asked.

The man didn't answer right away. He looked out to the water, among the boat wreckage and dark water. "I don't know," he said. "We just have to hope that doesn't happen."

The nervous look on Bo's face made it clear that he wasn't a fan of this answer. Still, he dutifully went back into the cabin, looking back to the ocean before he did so.

"Okay," the other man said. "I'm Carl and this is my boat, more or less. Can I get your names?"

"Emily."

"Steve."

"Good to meet you," Carl said. "I wish it were under different circumstances. But let's try to make the best of it, okay? Let's get you inside, up to the cabin."

He offered his hand to Emily and she took it, getting to her feet. She also felt Steve's hand at her elbow, helping her up. His touch was reassuring but still trembling. Carl led them into the cabin, which was much larger than the one inside the boat Cliff had rented. Everything was tidy, although some things had been scattered to the floor in the close call with the megalodon moments ago. Just thinking about it made Emily anxious beyond comprehension, sure that the monster would come up from the depths at any moments and hit the boat with full force from underneath.

From the central cabin space, they went up a flight of stairs that Emily assumed would take them to the bridge. She took the stairs cautiously, her knees still wobbly and her nerves still feeling as if they were dancing on an electric wire.

"You okay?" Steve whispered from behind her.

"Yeah," she said. "I will be."

In the cabin, Carl pointed to a bench-like seat along the far wall. It was bordered with a series of computer screens that filled the cabin with an eerie glow. Emily saw that the man was visibly shaken. She wondered if he had been close friends with the man that had just been killed.

Bo was on the radio, scanning for a frequency and having no luck. "I don't know what's going on," Bo said. "Maybe it's the storm?"

"It's just rain, not a storm," Carl said. "Keep trying."

He approached the helm and reached out for the gear shift. Before his hand fell on it, though, he gave Bo a worried look.

"Did you shut it off?" he asked. "I thought it was in neutral when we stopped."

"It was," Bo said, his voice flat.

"What's wrong?" Steve asked.

Carl didn't answer. He pressed a few buttons and then messed with the gear shift. Emily watched it all in a daze, feeling like she was in a bad dream. And even though she was nearly zoned out from the shock of everything that had happened, she knew what was going on before Carl spoke it out loud.

"The engine is dead," he said, slapping his hand hard against the dash that ran along the length of the helm.

"Are you kidding me?" Steve said with a hysterical edge to his voice.

"No. Something must have happened to it when that damn shark hit us."

Emily easily recalled the popping and cracking noises she had heard when the megalodon had breached to take Zoe down. It had been a violent shake even thought it had been accidental on the shark's part.

"What do we do then?" Bo asked.

Carl took a deep breath and looked out to the ocean through the windows. He rubbed nervously at his head, as if trying to force away an oncoming headache. "Now I go down and see what happened to the engine. And you keep trying to place a distress call on the radio."

"Got it. Be careful."

"Yeah," Carl said, but his voice had a tremor in it.

He started for the stairs but stopped to look at Emily and Steve. "How many were in your boat?"

"Four," Emily said. "The driver was killed long before you guys showed up. Then there was Zoe and now…just us."

"We'll get you somewhere safe," Carl said. It was an empty comment, one that felt like a stirring of cold air within the cabin.

He left them with that and then headed back down the stairs. Emily felt herself wanting to break and hated herself for it. More than that, she hated the fact that as she started to weep, she buried her head into Steve's shoulder. When he put an arm around her for support, she sagged against him and cried like a baby.

Through her tears, she could just barely hear the useless static of the radio as Bo tried to find a clear channel. Between that, the rain and the droning sound of the sea, Emily wondered if this was what Hell sounded like.

11

With her face pressed against Steve's chest and the tears still streaming, Emily thought back to the first time she'd ever seen him. It was in an American Poetry class, something she had taken just as a breeze course to help keep her grades up. But Steve had been very much into the class, engaging in discussions during every single class. Emily had spotted him sitting in the quad on campus, sitting alone with nothing but a book.

Even now, she wasn't sure why she'd approached him. Maybe it had been pity. It might have also been the vague interest she had in him. She was not attracted to him, but she had appreciated the way he cared so deeply about the written word. So she had approached him one day with a simple "hey."

He'd looked up with a nervous smile that spoke of inexperience in speaking with the opposite sex. "Hey," she said. "Emily, right? From American Poetry."

"Yeah. Look, I just wanted to say how much I really enjoy your arguments with Professor Towles. It's the highlight of that class for me."

"Thanks," he said. "Not a fan of poetry?"

"No. Honestly, I needed the grade. And it's an easy class."

"It is," he agreed.

"Anyway, I just wanted to say hi," she said. "I'll see you around."

She took two steps before he stopped here. When he did, it was with a shaky voice. "Do me a favor?" he asked.

"Maybe," she said, turning hesitantly around.

He reached into his book bag, sitting by his feet and pulled out a small paperback book.

"What's this?" she asked.

"Poetry by a guy named James Tate. You won't hear about him in class. Maybe you just need to read the right kind of poetry."

"Thanks," she said, having no intention of reading it. Still, when she took the book from him, she caught…*something* in his eyes. Maybe there was something there…maybe there was some hidden chemistry between them. Or maybe she was just vibing on the quiet, mysterious guys that seemed to be pretty intelligent.

She'd returned the book two classes later and *had* read some of it. She found it clever but, at times, a bit pretentious—which was funny because that's how she felt about Steve when all had been said and done.

Emily lost herself in that whirlwind of memories as the very same person she was regretting held her. As she realized the grim irony in this, she heard a crackle of static and then a voice that boomed loudly through the cabin.

"We read you, but just barely."

Emily looked up and saw that Bo looked relieved. He pressed the button on the side of the mic and responded. "Thank God," he said. "We're on a research vessel about thirty miles off the coast. We've recovered two survivors from a brutal shark attack and need assistance fast."

"Roger that," came the response. "Can I please have the vessel's identifiers?"

"Ah, yeah. Let me hand you over to the captain." Bo cast Steve a helpless look and said, "Can you run down and get Carl?"

Steve looked hesitant at first but, apparently understanding that this was a situation where he could actually be of use, got up and headed for the stairs. He looked back to Emily and said, "I'll be right back."

She nodded, cringing internally at how sincere he was trying to sound. Still, she found herself standing up and looking down the stairs, waiting for him to come back. She stared down the stairs and could hear the rain intensifying against the boat. It rocked gently, barely enough to feel as she stood in the cabin.

Less than twenty seconds later, Steve appeared, headed up the stairs with Carl behind him. Carl rushed right past her and took the mic from Bo. Emily tried to listen, but Steve was instantly in her ear, speaking softly.

"I think this could be very bad," Steve said lightly.

"Why?" she asked, also talking quietly.

"When I got down there, Carl looked like he'd seen a ghost or something. He's scared. I think the engine is really messed up."

Emily said nothing. She tried to eavesdrop on the conversation that Carl was having with the people on the radio, but the fear of being stranded out here with that monster somewhere in the depths around them was just too distracting. She caught bits and pieces of it, her eyes constantly drawn to the unforgiving black ocean in front of them.

"Hey."

Emily blinked her eyes in surprise, realizing that Carl was speaking to her.

"Sorry," she said. "Zoned out."

"It's quite alright," Carl said. "You've been through a hell of a lot."

"So what's the deal?" Steve asked from beside her. "I heard the guy on the other end mention something about the Coast Guard. Is that right?"

"Yeah," Carl said. "There's a coast guard helicopter out running routine drills about eighty miles away from here. They're going to contact them and have them re-direct our way. They should show up within half an hour."

"And what about the engine?" Emily asked. She was afraid to ask but she felt like she *had* to. She had felt herself slipping into a fugue sort of state—a state where she would totally blank out and becoming useless. She was not going to do that in the face of danger especially not with Steve here, jumping at every chance to be her knight in shining armor.

"From what I can see, it's cracked," Carl said. "We're also spewing gas out into the water. It's essentially dead."

"So we're stranded then?" Steve asked.

"Yes."

The cabin fell into silence as that information weighed down on them. The four of them exchanged uneasy looks before Bo broke the silence.

"So what do we know about this thing?" Carl asked. "This…*shark.*"

"Well, I don't think it's a simple shark for starters," Emily said. "The thing we're seeing easily beats the length of even the largest great whites ever recorded."

"How do you know?" Carl asked.

"I'm working on my Masters in Environmental Science," she said. "I almost decided to minor in Marine Biology but decided against it."

"So you know about sharks then?" Bo asked.

"Some, yes."

"So what the hell is that thing?" Carl asked.

"Well, there have been rumors of a few megalodons still floating around. No one likes to talk about it, but there *is* some evidence, though it's a bit sketchy."

"You mean the prehistoric shark?" Carl asked.

"Yes."

"I thought that was just a fable…like science fiction crap."

"Most people do," Emily said. "I did myself until about four hours ago. I don't know what else fits. I can't think of what else it could be."

Steve tried reaching out to take her arm gently, but she pulled it away. He looked at her, genuinely surprised. "You really believe that?"

"You've seen what it can do," she said. "You've seen how big it is. What else can it be?"

"She's right," Bo said. "I've seen a few great whites up pretty close. This thing is something different."

Carl rubbed at his head. "Okay," he said. "Assuming that we *are* talking about some kind of monster from the past, what do we know about it?"

"I think it's working on the same sort of principles a great white would," Emily said. She was fascinated by how quickly she was coming around now that she could put her knowledge to use. With her brain kicking into gear and having strangers relying on her for some sort of hope of survival, the tendency to slip away into a catatonic state was gone.

"What do you mean?" Carl asked.

"Like, when it took out our driver, and Zoe, and your other crew member, they were in the water and swimming as fast as they could to get away. Sure, it's never safe to be in the water with a shark but they are more prone to attack when they see you moving or hear a commotion."

"So stay quiet then," Carl said. "I think we can manage that."

"Wait," Steve said. "If that's the case, then why'd the damned thing come after us in the first place?" He turned to Carl and Bo, explaining how things began; he told them about seeing a blip of the depth finder that they assumed was a blue whale, only to find the megalodon breaching and, soon after, attacking their ship.

"That, I don't know," Emily said. "It almost seemed like it was hunting. Maybe if it had killed something near here before, it just assumed anything of a large size is food."

"Well that doesn't make me feel any better," Carl said.

"It would sort of align with that whale we saw, though," Bo pointed out.

"What whale?" Emily asked

"We saw this enormous sperm whale floating on the water," Carl answered. "It was clear that something big had taken it down."

Emily thought on this for a moment and then shook her head in disbelief. "We were out here looking for poachers," she said. "An alarming number of dead whales were showing up and no one was sure why. The reports all just assumed it was poacher activity. Maybe it was this megalodon all along."

"Well, if that's the case," Carl said, "we're floating right in the middle of its hunting ground."

"I suppose it makes sense in terms of survival," Emily said. "Even in areas where sperm whales are known to live, their numbers are scarce. If there's a megalodon that's looking for meals in an area where its food supply is getting limited, it would go after anything it thought might be appetizing."

Again, silence filled the cabin. It was unnaturally quiet and even the rain seemed to have lost some its strength even though it continued to fall outside. Emily thought that it was like knowing a bomb might be hidden in the boat and could go off at any moment. Knowing that the shark could be lurking anywhere nearby and had the potential to strike at any moment made her feel like she could jump out of her skin.

"So," Carl said. "It seems like all we can do is to stay as quiet as possible until the Coast Guard gets here."

"Are there any weapons on board?" Steve asked.

"There's a single pistol stowed away in a safe under that bench," Carl said, pointing to the seat behind Bo. "We have it on board in the event of piracy situations and, quite frankly, I don't think it would do any good against the thing I saw in the water ten minutes ago."

"So we wait," Bo said, his voice laced with nerves.

"We wait," Carl agreed, looking out to the dark water as if he feared that they might float off the face of the earth at any moment.

12

Time dragged on. They sat in the cabin as quietly as possible. They discussed any other safety precautions they could rely on (there were none, they found after those discussions), speaking in a whisper.

"Any idea why it just sort of disappeared on us?" Bo asked.

No one answered right away, but Carl ventured a guess. "The back end of the boat was hit pretty hard. And from what I could see, it just hit the boat with the lower half of its jaw. If it hit the blades on the propeller, it could have really hurt it."

"It *did* look a little dazed when it…" Steve said. "Well…when it came back up after it took Zoe."

They all chewed on this for a moment and fell quiet again. Emily didn't think she had ever felt the progression of time moving so slowly.

When the radio blared to life all of a sudden, all four of them were visibly frightened; a low-pitched shriek nearly escaped Bo's mouth, coming out in a hiccup sort of sound.

"MarineEx Vessel AS781, you still copy?"

Carl got up from his seat—the bench where he had indicated the gun was located—and picked up the mic. "Yeah, we're here."

"We just got confirmation that the Coast Guard helicopter is now exactly seventeen minutes out from your position. They were held up a bit due to the weather, but they are on their way."

"Roger that," Carl said. "And thanks."

"Just let us know of any further events that might occur between now and when the Coast Guard arrives."

"Got it."

When silence once again fell over them, it felt heavy this time. It was like a horror movie where the absolute stillness of everything seemed to invite the monster. It was driving Emily nuts and she couldn't stand it.

"I barely got a glimpse of your boat when we were pulled on," she said. "What's that contraption on the side of the boat?"

"It's a vacuum system that we use as part of our deep sea mining operation," Carl said.

"How long have you been out here?" Steve asked.

"This was the second day of a three day stint," Bo answered.

"What kind of stuff are you mining for?" Emily asked.

Carl gave a nervous grin. "The pump system and deep sea rovers we are using are an experiment of sorts. It hasn't really been cleared for use. As such, we can't really tell you too much about what we're doing."

"Those big things on the back of the boat," Steve said. "Those were the rovers?"

"Yeah. But, really…I can't discuss it."

Emily let out a laugh and rolled her eyes. Such secrecy seemed a little foolish, given their current predicament.

Bo got up from his seat and headed for the stairs. Even before he took the first one, Carl sat up, his eyes wide and alarmed.

"Where are you going?"

"Just to the galley," he said. "I figure our guests might need some water after everything they've been through."

"That would be great," Emily said.

"Yeah, thanks," Steve said.

He inched a bit closer to Emily and she paid no mind. She wondered if this was him trying to seem protective to her or to come off as being her boyfriend in front of these two older men. She figured it made no sense to get upset about it. If this was how needed to deal with the stress of the situation, she'd let him have it. It was the least she could do after he had saved her life twice in one afternoon. Also, if they planned on making it out of this alive, she was going to have to get over her annoyance with him. Besides…she hadn't been annoyed with him fifteen minutes ago when she had been balling her eyes out on his shoulder, had she?

Bo came back up the stairs with four plastic bottles of water. Steve took two from him, immediately uncapping one and handing it to Emily. She took it gratefully and drank it, not realizing how thirsty she was until the water was down her throat. She forced herself to stop drinking, fearful that she might get a cramp.

"Ugh, I can't stand just sitting," she said. She got to her feet and approached the front of the cabin, looking out of the window. The sea was actually quite beautiful in the moonlight, despite the remaining stray bits of wreckage from the boat that had carried her out here. Still, despite the near-serenity she felt by looking at the water, there was the fear that it could be broken by the sudden sight of an immense dorsal fin.

She finally made herself look away. She turned to Steven and saw that he was looking directly at her. He didn't bother breaking his stare when she caught him. He gave her a nervous smile which she did not return.

Before things could get any more awkward, the radio broke the silence again. "MarineEx Vessel AS781, come in, please."

Carl took the mic and replied, "This is MarineEx Vessel AS781."

"This is Coast Guard Rescue Chief Hamlett," the same voice replied. "We're nearing your location but the rain is making it hard to see clearly. Could you please cut on a deck light or a search light?"

"I thought of that," Carl responded, "but didn't want to give this shark anything to come charging at."

"I understand that loud and clear," Hamlett said. "Do you have a flare gun?"

"I do."

"Head out to the top of your vessel and fire it off into the air. Wait about three minutes before doing so, though. We're still about ten miles away."

"Will do. And Chief Hamlett?"

"Yes?"

"This shark…well, it's something else. I don't even know how to explain it. Just please use caution."

"We always do, I assure you. See you in a bit. Just hold tight."

Emily listened to the entire conversation and knew that she should be relieved—maybe even happy. But instead, all she could see was that monstrous face coming out of the water, the dark eyes of some long-forgotten leviathan from the deep. She'd seen it take three people already and for some reason that her heart could not understand, she didn't think she was going to get away from it so easily.

13

Without asking, Emily assumed that Carl had been the man in charge of their experimental little journey. She could sense it in the way Bo responded to him and how Carl himself seemed to take initiative for everything. It was obvious that he was nervous as he walked below to retrieve the flare gun but he moved like a man with a purpose—a man that would not be swayed from his duties.

"Need any help?" Steve asked as Carl headed down the stairs.

"No thanks," Carl said. "You guys stay inside. Stay safe and hold tight."

Steve seemed relieved to hear this answer. He was once again standing directly by Emily and she was pretty sure that he was clumsily trying to take her hand. She nearly reached out and took it—for comfort and to placate him in the moment—but ended up moving to the other side of the cabin instead. She looked out into the night again, waiting for the red streak of Carl's flare to arc through the sky. She thought of the last flare she had seen and how terrified she had been, floating in the ocean with an eighteen year old that would be dead less than three hours later.

That hadn't been too long ago and although she was in a somewhat better position now, the threat was still the same. And it all came down to a flare again.

When Steve scurried up beside her, she ignored him at first. She kept looking out, waiting for the flare.

"I'm sorry," Steve said quietly.

Emily looked at him, perplexed. "Sorry for what?" she asked.

"Being obsessive," he said. And now, for the first time since she could remember, he wasn't looking at her. He looked to the floor after his apology. "I know I have been and I know your reaction to me over the last few months has been warranted. I never meant for it to be like this. I liked you right away. Even before you approached me in the quad and I gave you that James Tate book. I just…I don't know. It sort of festered. Even when I knew you were being as polite to me as you could by not telling me to get lost, I kept going. So, I'm sorry."

"You're a good guy, Steve," she said. "And yeah, I think obsessive is the right word to use. But why in God's name are you telling me all of this *now?"*

"Because of what we've been through," he said. "Call it macho or whatever you want, but I want to make sure you're safe. I know you can take care of yourself. I have no doubt about that. But I care for you and want to help keep you safe. That's out of genuine *caring*…not that dumb obsessive part of me."

She was fairly sure he was being genuine and it made her feel much more comfortable about being in this horrifying situation with him. She smiled at him and tried to think of what to say but before she could form a word, the flare went off.

It arced to the right, a perfect little stream of flame that went upwards in a U-shape and then came scaling back down towards the night-streaked water. As soon as the flare had died out, they could hear Carl's footsteps coming back down towards the main cabin. When he came trundling up the stairs, he was wet with rain and looked pale.

"You okay?" Bo asked.

"For now," he said. "I saw its fin. About thirty yards out. I barely saw it and shot the flare in that direction just to be sure. It was there. I hope the flare may have distracted it."

"It was still out there?" Emily asked.

"Yeah," Carl said. "It's almost like it was waiting for us—like it knew we had to move eventually."

"Are sharks that smart?" Steve asked.

"Most are, yeah," Emily said.

"Well, if it knows the boat is here, why doesn't it just plowing into us like it did with Cliff's rental?" Steve asked.

"I don't know," Emily said. She wondered if the megalodon had some sort of base prehistoric drive where it enjoyed the hunt as well as the meal itself. She'd never heard of such a thing but then again, she also hadn't believed megalodons existed up until about four hours ago.

"Here's a question," Bo said. "If we're supposed to be quiet to keep it from attacking us, how do you think it will respond when a helicopter starts hovering directly above us?"

"I was thinking the same thing," Carl said. "I just didn't want to say it out loud and scare the hell out of everyone."

"We should all be out on the roof before we even hear the helicopter," Emily said. "That way we'll at least see if the thing comes for us."

"Sounds good to me," Bo said, already heading for the stairs.

"Life jackets are down in the galley, under the bench seats," Carl said as they started down the stairs. "There are emergency beacon lights, too. But maybe we shouldn't use those in this case."

"Probably not," Emily agreed as they came into the galley.

All four of them got a lifejacket and suited up right away. They then ventured out onto the stern and made their way quickly and quietly up the metal ladder than led to the top level of the boat. The rain was coming down harder than it had been when Emily and Steve had come aboard and it made it hard to see clearly.

Bo went up first, followed by Emily, then Steve with Carl bringing up the rear. When they reached the top, Emily nearly lost her footing due to the slick surface. When she regained traction, she couldn't help herself; she looked out to the right, looking for any sign of the megalodon. She saw nothing more than the black waves of the sea at night. Seeing it stretch out endlessly beneath her was dizzying and she had to look away.

She then looked down to the back of the boat. The damage the shark had caused was visible but not obvious. There was a very obvious upward buckle in the deck and one of the rear rails had come dislodged. Two of the six ROVs that Steve had asked about seemed to have come unfastened from the latches that apparently held them to the boat. She also saw the vacuum that Carl had been so secretive about attached to the side of the boat, and wondered how much the machine might be worth. If the megalodon tore through *this* boat, how much money would be lost? She'd seen the computers and other electronics inside, so she assumed the loss of this boat would mean a significant monetary hit to whoever MarineEx was.

Emily reached out behind her, found Steve's hand, and took it. He accepted it eagerly as they all looked up through the rain, waiting for the helicopter. She looked in the other direction and saw the debris from their boat. It was strewn everywhere and some pieces had likely sunk to the bottom of the ocean, having taken on too much water.Her train of thought was derailed when she heard a noise that was almost like what she imagined machine gun fire must sound like. It was coming from her left and when she turned in that direction and saw the distant white light in the sky, her heart dared to hope. Maybe they *were* going to make it out of this alive after all.

The noise became clearer—the sound of the approaching Coast Guard helicopter. As the white light got closer, the shape of the helicopter could be see through the night and the rain. It started to descend as it got closer, its light falling on the MarineEx boat.

"Hell yeah," Steve said under his breath. Emily saw him take one nervous look back to the water, as if he was certain that this easy rescue was too good to be true.

The helicopter came directly over the boat, the cyclic motion of the blades causing the rain to fall around them in bizarre patterns that felt like sleet on their faces. It churned overhead and, to Emily, sounded like looped mechanical thunder. She wondered how it might sound to the megalodon, potentially waiting for its chance to strike underwater.

When the helicopter was positioned over the boat, no more than twenty feet overhead, a single line was thrown down. It uncoiled like a snake, in the spotlight along the side of the helicopter. It missed the edge of the boat by about a foot and when it was completely straightened out, a man came to the edge of the helicopter side door and looked down. The helicopter moved a bit, dragging the line over a bit. When it struck the edge of the boat, it made a solid sound, almost metallic.

Without much hesitation, the man came down the cable quickly. It was hard to see from the rain and the lack of light, but Emily thought that he was attached to the cable with some sort of pulley-like device. When he was halfway down, a second man came out over the edge of the door and started down the cable as well. This one came down with what looked like a large steel basket beneath him.

The first man was down in less than ten seconds. He was dressed in a black skin-tight suit and wore protective eye gear. When he spoke, he did so in a shout so he could be heard over the rain and the whirring of the blades twenty feet above them.

"Is anyone injured?" he asked.

The four of them answered in the negative. They were all looking into the sky, eager to get to the safety of the helicopter.

"Okay. Then we're going to take you up in the basket two at a time."

By then, the second man had arrived. He was checking the hooks that connected the basket to the cable, making sure they were good and secure. With a nod of satisfaction, he stepped out of the way.

Carl nodded to Emily and Steve. "You guys first," he said.

Emily stepped forward towards the basket. As the second man reached out to help her in, she could hear a very faint voice coming from an earpiece in the man's ear. It was so small that she had not seen it until now.

She couldn't hear what the tiny voice said, but whatever was said alarmed the man right away.

"What is it?" Carl asked.

"Something in the water," the man said, turning to look.

Everyone else turned that way as well. In the dark, it was hard to see the dorsal fin clearly, but it was there. It looked like a moving whitecap of one of the waves, coming at them with incredible speed. As it neared them, it seemed to grow taller until the massive back of the megalodon started to show.

"Shit!" Carl screamed. "Hold on to something!"

But even as he shouted this, the command fell dead in the air. They were on top of the boat and there was nothing to hold on to.

"In the basket, now!" the rescue diver shouted. He grabbed Emily's arm and drug her forward.

She got one leg in and was swinging the other one over into it when the shark struck the side of the boat. It felt like a small explosion as the entire starboard side of the boat pitched violently to the side. A cacophony of screams pounded out over the rainfall and helicopter noise. Emily felt the metal basket slide out from under her leg. She went airborne for a moment and then struck the roof of the boat. The air went spiraling out of her lungs in a painful gasp but before she had time to register this, she felt herself slipping.

The boat was now canted at an angle, the shark still engaged with it. Emily reached out for the basket but missed it. As she scrambled for purchase, one of the rescue divers was able to grab her arm and stop the slide. He helped her to her feet as there was yet another violent shaking of the boat. This time there was a massive surge to the side, as if the shark were a cat and the boat was nothing more than a ball of yarn.

The first rescue diver that had come down the cable went sailing, falling over the side. He fell into the dark water below as Emily finally started to get a sense of the situation. Not only was the first rescue diver gone, so were Steve and Carl.

The second rescue diver was frantically pulling at the basket, trying to get it straight. Overhead, the helicopter was working to get re-positioned. The moving light had a nearly strobe-like effect that made Emily wince.

Finally, the boat stopped moving. It was at an angle, as the starboard side was essentially destroyed. Three of the six ROVs had become dislodged and splashed into the water. That side of the boat was at a massive slant of splinters and beams. Emily figured that as that side took on more water, the boat would basically flip over, revealing its port side to the sky.

"Where's Steve?" she asked the diver. Of course, he had no idea who Steve was and only shrugged. "We have to get you off of this boat."

She nodded, but felt like she was floating into a very bad dream. She reached out for the cable attached to the basket and steadied herself as best she could. She was only now able to drawn breath into her lungs and her back was miserable. She saw a focused look come to the diver's face and when he pressed a finger to his ear, she knew that he was getting more information from the helicopter pilot.

"The shark seems to have gone away for the moment," he said. "Get in the basket while you can."

"But the others…"

"I'll do what I can, but I have to take you one at a time. You're here now, so *you* get in."

"Okay," she said, feeling guilty at the relief that passed through her.

She got into the basket and the moment she was securely in, the cable tightened and she felt herself being hauled upwards. The higher she was pulled up, she was given a better view of the turmoil below her.

The entire starboard side of the ship was a mess; there was a visible hole that was large enough to drive a car through. Pieces of it were littering the water, mingling with the wreckage of their original rental boat. She also saw two people in the water—the first rescue diver and Carl. She looked around for Steve and saw that he had apparently fallen from the roof and landed on the back of the boat. He was getting to his feet as she looked down and she saw a noticeable hobble in his step. On top of the boat, Bo and the second rescue diver had still managed to remain in place. Bo was clinging to one of those small rails along the sides, crouching on his knees.

She then looked up to the helicopter. There was another ten feet or so before she'd reach the safety of the interior. It hung in place overhead, its rooters slicing through the rain, almost teasing her. She looked back down, hoping that they'd all have time to be rescued. The boat, while damaged, was still managing to stay afloat relatively well and there were—

In a flash, the surface of the water directly to the right of the boat seemed to explode. Emily shrieked as she saw the gaping mouth that surfaced, coming upwards like a projectile. The bastard had gone back below and sped towards the surface, coming up to breach and potentially destroy the boat. Earlier, they had discussed the possibility that this thing was hunting. But as she considered the spite and strength the megalodon was putting into making sure it did its best to kill them all, Emily couldn't help but wonder if there was something inherently evil to it. Maybe it was a territorial thing, some base instinct to protect its home.

She shook the thought aside. It wouldn't do her any good to try to rationalize its actions. Yes, it was a mysterious creature that no one had ever experienced before, but right now it was trying to kill her. She could waste time trying to figure out its nature when she was back on land—if she ever made it back on land, of course.

As she watched it rise up from the water, she feared that the basket was going to be snatched right out of the air in its jaws. But as more of its body tore through the water and into the air, she realized that it was coming up on the other side of the helicopter. It wasn't the boat the shark was after—it was trying to bring the helicopter down.

She knew that the shark did not have the mental capacity to realize that the helicopter was here as a means of rescue; it simply wanted to take down the noisy intruder. It made her think that maybe the megalodon *was* trying to protect the area it thought of as its home.

Similar to what it had done before taking out *The Gull*, the shark's entire body came out of the water and made a bent U-shape. It snapped its jaws at the helicopter and, despite its length, came up just a bit short. Emily breathed a sigh of relief, nearly collapsing into the basket.

But then its tail came around to finish out that U shape, slapping around in a natural descent and following the weight of the rest of its body back down to the water. When it did, the tail slapped the side of the helicopter. Emily could hear the cracking noise from the basket.

That wasn't the worst of it, though. The shark's tail got hung in the landing feet of the chopper. *Skids,* Emily thought. *Those are called skids.* She nearly laughed like a maniac at how that random bit of trivia popped up in her terrified mind. She was aware that this had happened several times in the last few hours and she wondered if it was simply her mind's response to times of severe trauma.

The trivial item of naming those lower rungs on the helicopter, like everything else in her mind and body, suddenly stopped being carried up as the weight of the shark pulled the helicopter down. *My God,* Emily thought as she screamed. *That bastard must weight a ton...*

But that thought and her screams were cut off as the basket hit the water. She barely had time to recover from the impact, the water splashing up around her and the shaky frame of the basket jarring her, before she could hear the squeals of the helicopter rotors going underwater. It was a wretched noise that tore through the noise of everything else. It sounded out behind her like some ancient beast from the depths, rising up to see what all of the commotion was about.

Emily felt herself being pulled under by the suction. She kicked off of the basket, stroking for the surface, but she could not move. She tugged her legs forward and found extra weight on them.

The cable, she thought. *The cable and the basket...my leg is wrapped to it. I'm trapped.*

She continued to try to free her leg as the ocean continued to swallow her and the sounds of chaos followed her down.

14

Her lungs started to ache and her heart felt like a caged animal trying to break free as her body desperately begged for air. She continued trying to free her leg, but there was no use; every time she pulled, the cable seemed to draw tighter against the basket. It was so tight that when the basket came to a sudden stop, striking against something and halting her descent, she felt a jarring in her bones. Even underwater, she could hear her teeth clink together. Her leg was pulled tight—so tightly that she feared that it might dislocate from her hip or at the knee at any moment.

In the murk of the dark ocean water, Emily could see flickers of fire in the violence all around her. Her head started to hurt and she felt light-headed as her oxygen supply reached its end. Her lungs seemed to be screaming and the only relief she had as she was sure there were less than a handful of seconds before she would drown, was that the basket had struck something—likely a portion of the helicopter. A moment of blinding hope flared up inside of her when she realized that she was no longer sinking straight to the bottom.

Still, even this small break was useless. The cable was too tight and she was disoriented. There was no way she could—

She felt something brush by her leg and she nearly expelled her last bit of breath in a scream of terror. She was sure the megalodon had come for her and for one terrible moment, she was relieved that she'd be swallowed whole by the beast and this entire stupid mess would be done. To drown or to be devoured by the shark…she didn't care. She was just done. She was tired. She was—

Her leg was suddenly free and there was a different sort of pressure against her. She felt something hook her under her arms and then she felt herself carried upwards. She could feel her lungs tightening, almost like they were being pinched shut. She felt a thrumming in her leg as the circulation returned to it and, though it all, the chaotic motion of the sea all around her.

Then somehow, out of nowhere, there was air. Emily gasped it in. It was painful at first, her lungs expanding and once again getting used to the air. She coughed as she took the air in, taking in some sea water as well. She gasped again and again, like someone choking, before her lungs seemed to remember what it was like to breathe.

"I got you," someone said from close by. It was this voice that helped her to realize that she was in the arms of one of the rescue divers. "Give me a minute…everything's a mess. I need to figure out how to—"

He stopped here and she wondered if it was because she'd heard the panic in his voice. Perhaps he was on the verge of losing hope and didn't want her to sense it.

"Donald!" The driver screamed the name so loud that it hurt Emily's head. She felt herself being pulled through the water quickly. She could hear weird screeching noise from beneath her; she assumed these were the muffled complaints of the downed helicopter as it continued to fall to the bottom of the ocean beneath her.

Slowly, she started to come around. The diver, still pulling her along, yelled that name again: "Donald!"

"Where is everyone else?" Emily asked.

"Scattered," he said. "I saw you go down so I went after you. We'll see what we can do about the others after I get you safe."

"But they—"

But the diver wasn't hearing it. He had reached the man he had been calling Donald. He looked to be treading water and fighting for his life. There was something attached to Donald's back and he seemed to be pulling it along as if it were a large knapsack.

Everything in the water around them was a mess. The debris of two boats and the abstract lights from below as the helicopter sank threw everything off. She was pretty sure Donald was pulling something behind him, though.

"This damned raft is tangled," Donald said. "And I can't reach the straps to untangle it." Emily could tell the man was terrified. She looked from the raft and then back to Carl's boat. It bobbed haphazardly, its damaged side having taken on enough water to make the ship tilt almost completely on its side. She saw someone—Bo, she thought—trying to swim slowly towards it.

"Shit," the diver said. Emily felt him trying to angle her in a way where he could reach Donald's pack without releasing her.

"It's okay," she said. "I can tread for a while."

"You sure?"

She wasn't, but as her body became less starved for air and her mind began to work clearly again, she understood the severity of the situation. "Yes. But not for long."

"Okay. If you get tired, just grab my shoulders."

He released her and instantly went to Donald's back. The moment Emily started treading, she began to look around for any sign of the shark. She wondered if perhaps the crashing of the helicopter had frightened it away. But this seemed stupid, especially since the shark was at least twice as large as the helicopter.

She looked back towards the boat and saw Carl at the top, managing to hold on to the small rails. He was looking frantically around for something and was yelling for Bo. So far, there was no sign of Steve or the other rescue diver.

She looked back to the diver that had saved her and saw that he had nearly untangled a strap that seemed to extend from the base of a pack that Donald had on his back to a secondary pack that floated about two feet away. It then struck her that Donald had referred to the pack as a raft. As she watched, the diver untangled the strap and then removed the pack from Donald's back.

The pilot and Donald then worked together to position the pack in a particular way. The pilot then pulled a small cord from the side and gave it a fierce tug. Without any sort of warning, the pack seemed to explode. The pack became a large inflatable raft in an instant, almost like a magic trick. It was a sizeable raft and when it expanded, it nearly smacked Emily right in the face. She instantly tried climbing into it but was not able to get a firm grasp.

"Hold on," the diver said, swimming to the side. He helped her up and she slid into the raft, noticing that the pilot was clambering in on the other side. As he fell into the raft, Emily saw that he had a large cut on his left leg. Blood was pouring from it, instantly staining the soft floor of the black raft.

Emily sat up and looked back out to the water. The diver was already swimming towards the boat where Bo was still in the water, headed for safety. Bo was swimming slowly and seemed to be disoriented. His head would go under for a moment and then resurface. He'd take a lazy stroke forward and then seem to forget where he was and what he was supposed to be doing.

When the diver finally reached Bo, the disorientation washed away immediately. The diver placed a hand on his shoulder and Bo started to scream. He thrashed around in the water and screamed for his life. Emily knew the feeling; he was sure that the briefest touch was the shark. But what Bo was doing bordered on hysteria. And the more he screamed and splashed around, the more terrified Emily became. It could easily catch the attention of the megalodon, wherever it might be.

As Emily watched, Bo finally started to settle down. But when he did, he started clinging to the diver in an almost reckless fashion. He was still speaking loudly and in panicked tones, but at least he wasn't screaming anymore.

After what seemed like an eternity, Bo seemed to come around, allowing the diver to actually help him. The diver supported him by taking one of his arms and assisting him along. They were within about twenty yards of the boat, headed in that direction. Emily wondered if they were going to collect Steve or if the diver was electing to use the boat as Bo's safety. There was easily enough room remaining in the life raft to hold another eight people or so but it was much further away.

She watched them swim towards the boat, Bo now taking strides on his own.

To her horror, she saw the water separate behind them. It was replaced by the bulbous head of the megalodon. It came up quietly and without much force, just bobbing up in an almost casual manner.

The diver must have heard it. He had enough time to turn around and lay eyes on the beast. He was less than three feet away from it when the shark made a single movement forward and yanked him and Bo under. The last thing Emily saw as the shark went back underwater were its jaws closing up over Bo, as if he was nothing more than a tiny little fish.

Emily collapsed back into the raft. She felt a shriek building up in her throat but she swallowed it down. She felt like she had done that far too often ever since *The Gull* had been attacked. She wasn't sure how much longer she would be able to do it.

Behind her, the pilot sat motionless and wide-eyed. From the looks of it, he'd seen the entire thing play out as well. He looked to be speaking to himself, but no words were coming out of his mouth. *It's nice to know I'm not the only one that might be losing their mind out here,* Emily thought.

The idea that she was safe in the raft was ludicrous but she still felt much more secure than she had been out in the water. She dared to hope that as long as they remained quiet, they could go untouched. And surely, since the helicopter had gone down, the Coast Guard would send someone else out to check on their crew when no one was responsive over the radio. That was Emily's hope anyway.

She turned to the pilot to ask him about this and was again faced with the sight of his wounded leg. She assumed he had cut it in the crash somehow. Seeing it, she also followed the trail of his blood. It was pooling in the floor of the raft but before it collected there, it was also streaked all over the side of the raft where he had climbed in.

That meant it was also on the exterior side as well—and out there in the water. She knew sharks could smell blood and it was the equivalent of a bull being taunted with a red cape.

Realizing this, Emily didn't feel safe at all.

This was truer still when, just a handful of seconds later, she saw the familiar sight of that impossibly large dorsal fin breaking the surface of the water about fifty yards away from them.

It was headed directly for the raft, and it was coming fast.

15

The fin came closer at alarming speed and Emily couldn't help herself. This time, she let her scream out. She frantically tried to think of a way out of this. For a moment, she considered waiting until the very last possible moment and jumping out of the raft. One of the very few things she knew about the massive shark was that its massive size seemed to affect the speed it was able to maneuver. Going straight ahead, it was fast—almost impossibly so. But when it needed to turn, say going underwater and redirecting itself as it had done when it had taken Cliff's boat out, it took some time. She wondered if she could jump out of the raft and have enough time to swim the forty or so yards to Carl's capsized boat.

She needed to decide fast; the fin was less than ten yards away and now there was more than the fin above water. She saw its massive back rising up as it brought the tip of its head out of the water.

"Move!" the pilot yelled from behind her.

Before she could obey, she felt him shove her down to the raft floor. She looked up and saw that he had a flare gun. She had only a moment to wonder where the hell it had come from— maybe from the helicopter or a small hatch within the raft that she had not yet spotted—before he fired it.

He fired it directly ahead, as if it were an actual gun. The flare jetted out at the same moment the shark reared its head up. It struck the beast just to the left of center, pinging its snout. The flare seemed to sprout more flames for just a moment before falling from its hide. It seemed to have the merest effect on the shark; it slowed just a bit and went back underwater. When it did, its head slammed against the side of the raft.

Emily felt the raft being overturned and used that fact as her deciding factor from her earlier speculation. Seeing that the shark was still headed in its original direction—which would have placed it behind their current location after tearing through the raft—she leaped in the opposite direction, towards Carl's boat.

When she hit the water, she also hit something else. It was solid and moving with great speed. It cartwheeled her across the water, actually getting her much closer to the boat than she could have hoped. When she stopped skipping across the water and started swimming for the boat, she glanced back quickly. She was fairly certain she had struck the shark's tail and it had slapped her almost nonchalantly. But now she saw that tail going underwater quickly, taking a nearly instant turning motion.

It was going under to whip back around and finish the job. Emily went under herself, hoping that swimming underwater might not cause as much of a commotion for the shark to come after. That, plus the fact that she'd be away from the pilot's blood in the water, gave her some hope that she'd make it to the boat before it even noticed her in the water.

Of course, after she got back to the boat there were still no guarantees. But for now, she'd take what she could get. She swam quickly but moved her limbs as little as possible. She gave long, hard strokes with her arms and barely kicked her legs. It was difficult, as the water was still choppy from the helicopter wreckage.

She came up for air, surprised to find that she had nearly reached the boat. A few more strokes got her to the edge. The boat was almost entirely turned on its side, the majority of the wrecked in now submerged. In the bit of the damaged portion that remained above water, she was saw one of the rails from the back of the boat. It had become dislodged and bent but was still attached to the boat. It hung down like a crooked ladder, almost *too inviting*. Further overhead, she could see the strange vacuum contraption that Carl had seemed so secretive about. It clung to the side of the boat and looked very heavy—additional weight she was sure the damaged boat absolutely did not need. As for the ROVs that had been so neatly nestled along the back of the boat, she saw no sign of them.

She reached up and grabbed the edge of what she assumed was the pump's base. The moment her hand was on it, she heard her name from above her. She peered up and saw Steve. He was looking down at her from the crooked floor of what remained of the un-submerged second floor deck where the central cabin had been.

"Quiet," Emily said. "Stay as quiet as you can."

He nodded his understanding and watched her, waiting for her to get far enough up to be of help. She climbed up the pump as well as she could, but there were very few flat surfaces to take advantage of. Still, once she got a firm grip around the top, she was able to use her feet along the side of the boat to make it up a good distance.

As she climbed up, there was a large splash from behind them. This was followed by a scream that she was unable to *not* turn around to investigate. She turned to see the megalodon splashing back down into the water. Its mouth missed the pilot that had been bobbing in the water a few feet away from the raft. When the shark hit the water and went down, so did the pilot. He disappeared underneath it, carried down by its weight.

"My God," Steve whispered. "He was crushed, he was—"

But then the pilot came back up again, still screaming. There was blood on his face and he looked like a phantom in the moonlight. His screams were cut off in a gurgling sort of sound as he was jerked violently to the left. He was pulled hard in that direction, going at an incredible speed. They watched him glide like that from the waist up for a few seconds before he sank lower and lower. Finally, he was pulled violently underwater, one final wail of agony that was cut off as his head went under.

After that, there was silence.

Emily whimpered and pulled herself up by the pump's base. Her arms were trembling and every muscle in her body begged for her to take a break and allow herself to weep—to become the vulnerable woman that had earlier sank into Steve's shoulders. She tried to push it aside, but she was crying by the time she was high enough up the side of the boat to reach out and take Steve's offered hand.

As he pulled her up and into the ruined and quickly disappearing central cabin, she saw Carl peering down at them from the stairwell. He had to lean against the opposing wall to keep from falling. Everything was skewed and out of place, so much so that it took Emily a few moments to get her bearings straight.

"You okay?" Steve asked

"No," she answered with a whimper. "But that's okay."

"Come on, you two," Carl said. "The more weight that I have down here, the worse off we are. Come in up to the top."

"Is there a plan to get to safety?" Emily asked. "I mean, what the hell are we supposed to do?"

"There's nothing now," Carl said. "I can only hope that the pilot was able to make some kind of distress call before the chopper went down."

"I was hoping the same thing," Emily said as they scrambled up the crooked stairs. She moved quickly and lost her balance twice but was able to make it onto the top of the boat—which was really the left side—without falling. "Someone will have to come looking for them when they don't respond, right?"

"I sure hope so," Carl said.

They gathered together on the edge of the boat. It was tricky, as they had to go out on the top of the boat and then take a sliding step back down to rest on the edge which, less than twenty minutes ago, had been mostly submerged under water in its normal state.

"Someone explain this to me," Steve said, his voice bordering on hysteria. "I know nothing about sharks but even I know that noise would probably attract them. So wouldn't a helicopter be the absolute worst thing to send for a rescue?"

"There's no way they could have known just how…how *monstrous* this thing is," Carl pointed out.

"With a simpler shark," Emily said, "they would have successfully rescued us."

The stared out to sea, taking in the situation. There was wreckage and debris everywhere. The black life raft bobbed like a shadow in the midst of everything, clinging to a piece of scrap from what she thought was a remnant of the deck from *The Gull*. She also saw what she thought was a portion of seat from the helicopter.

She felt like she was riding on a storm cloud. Everything was dark and brooding. There was no hope anywhere. The only hope she was able to muster was the fact that she could see no signs of the megalodon.

But she had seen just how quickly it could come to the surface, its maw opened wide to tear into anything over its head. She knew that she could be dead at any moment; there may as well have been a sniper out there somewhere with her head in his scope.

"So," Carl said. "I guess the game plan is to just stay quiet and hope the Coast Guard sends someone else?"

"That seems like the only thing we *can* do," Emily said.

She felt exhaustion sinking in and when Steve scooted next to her, she resisted the urge to rest her head on his shoulder. Feeling not only alone, but in desperate need of some sort of comfort, she reached out and took his hand. He looked at her, confused, but said nothing. He gave her hand a reassuring squeeze, but she could still feel the tremors going through him—or maybe the tremors were her own. She couldn't tell.

The tepid silence between them didn't last long. It was broken by a mechanical shrieking that sounded totally alien out here on the sea. It took roughly three seconds for her to realize what she was hearing: it was an alarm of some sort.

"What is that?" she asked.

"The pump alarm," Carl said, already heading carefully back to the edge of the boat where he looked down into the wreckage below. "It must be shorting out due to all of the water."

"Can you shut it up before that thing comes back?" Steve asked.

"I can try," Carl said, but he looked worried.

"What is it?" Emily asked. "What's wrong?" She had to raise her voice over the noise of the alarms.

"With the water coming into the boat the way it is, I don't know that I'll be able to shut it off. And even if I can…well, I'll probably get electrocuted."

"How bad?" Steve asked.

"I have no idea."

Carl gave a sigh and then turned away from them. He stepped down onto the lower level and slipped inside an area where a window had once looked out to the sea. Carefully angling himself into the tilted shattered window, he lowered himself down into the flooded remains to what had once been the central cabin.

"Wait," Emily said. "Carl, let's try to think this through."

The only response she got was that shrill beeping, an alarm that seemed to be getting louder. It pounded into her head and it felt as if the alarm was actually doing nothing more than alerting the megalodon to the fact that it had left a few straggling survivors behind.

16

"So let's plan for this," Steve said.

"Plan for what?" Emily asked.

They stood face to face with less than a foot between them, but the way he stood by her made it clear to her that he meant to protect her if anything should happen. The rain had weakened to little more than a drizzle and Emily realized that she could hear the sound of the ocean clearly now—that rhythmic and almost eternal sort of breathing.

"If he gets electrocuted down there...if he dies...what the hell are we going to do?" he asked. "Yeah, we can wait for the Coast Guard to show up again, but that didn't really go so well last time, now did it?"

"I don't know," Emily said. She was still holding his hand. He had a grip on it that made her think he didn't plan on releasing it anytime soon.

As it turned out, though, they didn't have to worry about coming up with a back-up plan. Less than a minute after Carl had gone down into the partially submerged boat below, the alarms came to a stop. They heard some brief scurrying from beneath them and then Carl's whispered voice from their right.

"Can I get a hand?" he asked.

They both carefully walked over to the area where the central cabin door was now completely sideways. Carl was walking along the wall now, arching his back to make it back out through the door.

"Take this for me, would you?" he asked Steve.

He handed over a large rectangular device that, to Emily, looked like a really sophisticated remote control for a child's remote-controlled car.

"What is it?" Steve asked.

"Well, if I know what I'm doing—and honestly, that's a bit of a stretch—that thing might be what saves us."

"Okay…"

It was clear that Steve wanted an explanation. Emily did, too. But she was willing to just let Carl go ahead with whatever plan he had. Even if it was an awful plan, doing *something* was better than standing idly by on the side of his boat, waiting for it to sink or for the megalodon to come back…whichever happened first.

"The alarms that went off were to tell me that one of the back-up systems for the vacuum is dead. That's not surprising, considering the state of the boat. But when I shut them down, I came up with an idea. And yes, I *did* get a little shock from messing with the computers. Stung like hell, but nothing lethal. But that little shock is what gave me my idea."

"And what is it?" Emily asked, now just wanting him to spit it out.

"That controller," he said, pointing to the thing still in Steve's hand, "is a manual way to operate the rovers."

"But they fell off the boat," Steve said. "How are they any good to us now?"

"They were made to be dropped into the ocean," Carl explained. "Sure, these weren't optimal conditions and one of them seems to have been damaged in all the hell that broke loose. But that leaves five that are still operational. I can still see them on the one screen inside that is still working. And if you look here," he said, tapping a button on the remote control and bringing up a small digital display, "you can also see them. So even if everything in the boat goes dark, those ROVs will still run until they get a shut-off command from this controller. Also, there's another device that fell off the boat that we call the Collector. It attaches to the pump and we lower it down. Only now, it's not attached. So it's just sort of down there. It's also still operational and landed almost directly beneath us."

"Okay…" Emily said, still not seeing where this was going.

"Anyway, like the vacuum and pump, the ROVs also have alarms. We built them in for testing procedures. Naturally, they'd do no good now, because they're on the bottom of the ocean and we wouldn't hear them."

"So why do we care about the rover alarms then?" Steve asked.

"Well, just because *we* can't hear them doesn't mean that certain things underwater can't hear them. In fact, the alarms are pretty damn loud. Our tests were in twelve feet of water; the alarms had to be loud so we could hear them above ground."

"So you're talking about a simple distraction if the Coast Guard shows up again?" Steve asked. "You want the shark to be snooping around somewhere else when—*if*, I guess—someone else comes to rescue us?"

"No," Carl said. "If I'm being honest, at the rate the boat is taking on water right now, I don't know that we'd be able to stay out of the water until another attempt is made. No, my plan is to use this controller to direct all of the ROVs around the Collector. I'll kick on the alarms with and when the shark attacks them, I'll switch on the Collector."

"Is the pump strong enough to hold that thing?" Emily asked.

"Not likely," Carl said. "Not for long, anyway. The Collector is really just a large vacuum cleaner, really. There's a miniature pump in it and that's where the majority of its strength comes from. The thing we have going for us, though, is that the pipe isn't connected." He pointed to the mechanical arm-like structure on the far end of the side of the boat. "When the pipe's not connected, the system isn't going to recognize it for a good twenty seconds or so. As such, it will work overtime as it tries to compensate for that extra suction. So it'll be a bit stronger than usual. At the very least, it will stop the shark for a few seconds— long enough for me to send the command to the auxiliary cutter ROVs. We use those rovers to clear the way for the smaller ROVs that do the real mining. If I can position them just right, the auxiliary cutters will tear into the bastard."

"How many of these auxiliary cutters are there?" Steve asked.

"Two. But the others ROVs, while not as heavily equipped with blades and other digging utensils, can still do some damage."

"Will it be enough to kill it?" Emily asked.

"If I give it full speed and power, the auxiliary cutter has enough strength to plow through three feet of sediment at a depth of about two feet deep. And if the Collector can hold the bastard for even three or four seconds—even if it just slows it down the smallest bit—if it *doesn't* kill it, it's going to hurt it pretty damn bad."

"And how will you know when the shark is attacking?" Steve asked.

"That's the part that sucks. I'll have to monitor it from inside the boat to see the feeds from the cameras built into the ROVs. And I don't know how much longer I'll have the one good screen to work with."

"So we need to do this now then, huh?" Emily asked.

"Yeah."

"Are you certain this will work?" Steve asked.

"No. If Trevor—the guy in charge of all of the tech—was still here, it might be pretty easy. But I'm not overly familiar with the ROVs, much less the equipment. This is like the backup quarterback coming in at the fourth quarter, expecting to come from about two touchdowns behind."

"Sounds promising," Steve said. "You a Patriots fan?"

"No...Chiefs."

"Terrible analogy, then," Steve said with a nervous laugh.

"I think you should go for it," Emily says. "It beats sitting around and waiting to see who comes for us first—the Coast Guard or the megalodon."

"You both agree to this?" Carl asked.

"Sure," Steve said. Emily nodded her approval.

Steve handed the controller back over to Carl. He did so very cautiously, now understanding the importance of the rectangular device. "Is there anything we can do to help?" Steve asked.

"Yeah. Try to get to that raft over there. If this works out, we're still going to need something else to float around on. I don't see the boat lasting any more than half an hour."

They looked out to the raft and saw it bobbing about five feet away from the side of the boat; it was still trapped between the wake from Carl's boat and the same plank that she had spotted earlier. It was the one promising looking thing out there in all of the dark water and destruction.

"We can handle that," Steve said. "Just give is a heads up when the shark is headed for the rovers."

"Will do," Carl said. He looked to the remote control device a bit reluctantly and then shrugged. "Okay. I'll know within about two minutes if this is going to work. I'll let you know as soon as I can."

Emily and Steve only nodded; Emily was still looking to the raft and remembering that the floor of it was coated in the helicopter pilot's blood. She also recalled how easily he had died and how unexplainably lucky she was to still be alive.

Something about that made her heart seem to swell. She had made it this far. The last serval hours had been an absolute nightmare but she was still here. She'd seen far too much death and was essentially facing up against a prehistoric monster. The fact that she was still alive clicked on some internal mechanism attached to her survival instinct and she was suddenly determined to get back to land in one piece.

"Let's just get it done," she said.

"Yeah, let's do that," Carl said. He then turned and headed back into the boat, holding to what had once been the outer wall—which now served as an extension of the roof in an upside down sort of way—for support.

"You okay?" Steve asked as Carl headed back inside.

"Yeah," she said. "I just wish there was more I could do."

She again found herself reaching out for his hand. Maybe staring death in the face for a night had made Steve seem like not such a bad guy. She assumed that, like her, he was seeing his ability to die at any moment as some sort of life-changing measurement of the sort of person he was.

"How about you?" Emily asked. "How are you holding up?"

"I'm scared," he said. "But other than that, I just want to get out of the ocean."

"I'm glad you're here," she said, the comment coming out of nowhere.

He grinned at her and said, "If I said I was glad to be here with you, I'd be lying."

They both laughed nervously as they waited for Carl to call out to them. Meanwhile, the raft swayed lazily several feet away and the ocean continued to churn endlessly against the side of the boat.

17

When Carl waded back into the central cabin, he had to pause a moment to get his bearings straight. The ceiling was now serving as the far right wall and the far right wall was now serving as the floor, which was completely covered in water. More water surged in through the doorway to the stairs. It also came into the cabin in the form of tiny little rivulets through the binding of the windshield to the body of the boat.

Roughly half of Trevor's control panel was still above water. There were two screens—one of which had gone completely black—and his laptop. The laptop was secured into a metal frame where all of the other equipment fed into it through some sort of router system that Carl didn't understand. He figured he could probably operate the system from the laptop. That, plus the remote, would have to do. If it got too complicated, it might be like the blind leading the blind but…well, he just had to hope. Hopefully, the hardest part was going to be positioning the ROVs. He'd only had about fifteen hours or so of simulated tests with the rovers (compared to Trevor's one hundred hours or more) but that was going to have to be enough.

On the plus side, with the controller and the laptop as his tools, there would be much less of a risk of electrical shock and he was far more comfortable with a laptop than the over-the-top technical systems that were even now continuing to be overtaken by the water that continued to pour in.

With the controller held up over his head (even though he knew that it was waterproof, as was much of the other equipment that was currently submerged), Carl slid into the water. It came up to his waist, making footing in the tilted room tricky to master. And although he knew the vast majority of the electrical equipment in the room was waterproof to some degree, he also knew that he could get badly electrocuted at any moment. He wondered which would be most painful: electrocution or being eaten alive by a shark.

"Let's act fast and not find out," he muttered to the room.

He made his way over to the console and loaded up the software that he had seen Trevor use so many times. Carl knew the basics of the programs and how to operate everything, so he had *some* level of comfort when he saw the interface. Seeing that the Collector was online but powered down, he brought up the command to start it. Before kicking it into gear, though, he also brought up the camera feeds on all six of the different rovers. They were all online and the five that had been unharmed by the events that had transpired over the last few hours were waiting for instruction. The sixth was completely unresponsive. He couldn't even find its current position with the software while the others were clearly represented with little green dots. He powered the working ROVs up and then looked to the controller once again.

When he saw that all of the rovers were responsive to the remote's commands, he started leading the first one directly over towards the Collector. The rover moved slowly, but they had all fallen next to one another. Better still was the fact that none of them seemed to be very far away from the Collector. As he moved the first one, Carl craned his head back and half-yelled up to the top.

"Everything is running and it looks like we're good to go. These ROVs are slow, though, so try to be patient."

There was silence for a while and then a slight commotion from up above. A few seconds later, he saw Emily come slipping into view on the far side of the glass that had once looked straight ahead out to the ocean.

"How much longer?" she asked.

"Five minutes, maybe?"

"I don't know if we have that much time," she said, her voice thin and scared. "It's come back."

"Where?"

"It's swimming around the area where the helicopter went down."

Carl did his best to think but the fear that invaded his heart was too much to bear. There was only one thing to do, anyway. It would be risky and could like out a dent in his already fragile plan. But he saw no other alternative.

"I can set these alarms whenever I need to," he said. "If it starts coming closer to us, stomp on the boat up above. I'll set the alarms early."

"Okay," she said. He saw that she was close to crying and suddenly felt far too responsible for her. She was a stranger but chivalry wasn't as dead as people thought. He felt an inherent need to rescue not only her, but Steve as well.

He watched her slip back out of her view, climbing back to the top (or, more accurately, the *side)* of the boat. Carl looked to the laptop screen as he directed the first rover over to the Collector. It was moving excruciatingly slow and as he watched the red dot that served as its location on the laptop screen, he was overcome with the idea that this plan of his was probably not going to work.

18

The megalodon was swimming in a large circle, remaining in the area where the helicopter had gone down. As Emily climbed back up after having filled Carl in, she spotted its dorsal fin easily. It moved slowly, like it had no real reason to be there—just to keep them scared and on their toes. Emily wondered, not for the first time, if it was really that smart or diabolical, or both.

The rain had stopped, but the surface of the side of the boat was still slick. She looked to the raft and, not for the first time, found the idea of seeking any sort of safety in it borderline ridiculous. She recalled how flimsy it had felt when she had shared with the helicopter pilot and didn't like the idea of hopping back into it. How long would they be expected to play leapfrog from one meaningless means of safety to the next? It seemed like utter madness.

Still, even she could tell that Carl's boat was sinking pretty quickly. She also knew that the more water it took on, the quicker it would sink.

After what felt like hours but was in actuality less than two minutes, she heard Carl's whispered voice. It was hard to hear because he was trying to remain as quiet as possible and the constant drone of the ocean almost drowned it out. All she could hear was a simple, *"Hey guys!"*

Emily and Steve walked closely together to where the edge dropped off to make way for the cabin's walls and the side deck that separated them. She felt Steve's hand on her arm and feeling that extra support made her a bit more confident in walking along the slick surface.

"Yeah?" Emily asked.

"I've got three of the rovers positioned directly next to the Collector. Once I get the other two situated, we're in business."

"How much longer?" Steve asked.

"Maybe three minutes."

"Okay."

They remained where they were and looked back out to the raft. "Any idea how we're going to get into that thing?" Steve asked.

"I'm thinking about just jumping. I'm pretty sure we could make it."

"You've got an athletic build, though," Steve said. "I'm about thirty pounds overweight and spent my extra time in the art rooms and computer labs in college. That's one hell of a jump for me."

"Then I'll jump in and bring it over to get you."

"How?"

"I don't know. I'll find something to help me paddle it over.

"No."

"That's how it's going to have to be. Look, you saved my ass at least twice already today. We can do this. Just trust me."

"Are you sure?"

"Yeah," she said. "It'll be okay. Besides, if those alarms are as loud as Carl says, I don't even think it's going to matter if you *do* fall in the water."

"Maybe so...but I'd rather not fall in if it's all the same to you."

Emily looked back out to the raft again and now it seemed like a longer jump than five feet. Maybe it was seven or eight. Or maybe the darkness and the movement of the water were making it hard to judge.

Carl's voice came wafting ghostlike towards them again. "Third one is in place. Going for the fourth one now but...well, I'm getting some popping noises in here and little shocks here and there."

"Get your ass out of there," Emily said.

"Another two minutes or so," Carl replied. "I'll be okay."

Emily wanted to argue further, but not being able to see him made her feel like she was responding to voices in her head. And with nothing more than a black abyss of death and mysteries all around her, that was not a comparison that she wanted to make.

Emily looked back out to the water, looking for the fin. It was no longer in the area of where the helicopter had gone down. In fact, she couldn't find it anywhere. It made her wonder if the megalodon had gone underwater to build up speed, its sights set on the ruins of Carl's boat.

That idea made her knees tremble and for reasons that made no logical sense to her, she found herself wanting to leap into the raft right then and there. Maybe she should; after all, wouldn't it make more sense for one of them to be in the raft when Carl gave his final go ahead to move?

"Steve," she said, her heart already starting to thrum in her chest.

"Yeah?"

"I'm going for the raft," she said.

"But we don't even know where the damn thing is."

"I know. But—"

"The fifth one is lined up," came Carl's forceful whisper.

With that news, Emily was not so keen to jump into the raft. It felt too much like an endgame scenario…and they didn't even know the rules of the game yet.

"So we're good to go?" Steve asked.

"Good to go."

Steve looked to Emily and she was unable to look past the caring in his eyes. He was scared for her, but there was something there beyond that—something beyond what she had pegged as an emotion that flirted with obsession. There was fear there, sure, but the other thing she saw in his stare made her feel confident and *almost* safe.

For one thing, it made her feel more confident in her ability to make the jump from the ship to the raft.

"Ready?" Carl asked from beneath them. He sounded like he was in pain and trying his best to hide it.

"Go for it," Steve said.

Emily stepped closer to the edge of what currently served as the boat's roof. Looking into the water, she was sure that the boat had sunk another foot or so in the last few minutes.

There was silence for a good ten seconds. Emily felt her knees bending almost instinctively as she angled herself along towards the raft. One moment, it looked like she could almost step into it and the very next moment, it seemed a mile away. She tried to focus on it, to somehow make herself see it as a stationary object, but the rolling water made it impossible.

"Alarms are all blaring," Carl reported. His voice was louder now and Emily was more convinced than ever that he was in pain.

"Carl, are you okay?" she asked.

"Yeah, just wait for my word…"

Emily looked to Steve, a concerned look on her face. "He's hurt," she said.

"Maybe, but we don't have time to check."

"But what if he—"

"Okay, I see it coming!" Carl's voice was excited now, although clearly pained. "I see it on the ROV cameras…it's coming in fast. Get to the raft now!"

There was desperation in his voice. It almost sounded like he was crying.

Still, Steve was right. There was no time to check on him. If their window of time was as small as Carl had said, then she'd already wasted too much of it.

With guilt already starting to invade her heart, she sprang off of the side of the boat, aimed directly at the raft. She felt herself arcing and then falling and for a moment, she was sure that she was going to miss it by about a foot. But then as she fell, the raft settled off of a small wave. Emily fell onto the side of it, half in and half out. She hit hard and, with the air rushing out of her stomach, bounced in an awkward flip into the raft.

She scrambled to her knees as quickly as she could. She looked back to the boat and her heart shuddered at what she saw. Steve was walking away from the edge of the boat, heading for the area where they'd watch Carl come and go from the lopsided cabin.

"Steve!"

He turned back to her and gave her a thumbs up and a smile. He then hunkered down on his knees and slid down onto the side deck and out of sight.

"Damn it," Emily screamed.

And once the scream had left her, she realized that she was utterly alone. The sea lapped at the raft and somewhere underneath her, a massive prehistoric shark was hopefully pursuing technologically advanced machines that could potentially kill it. She felt something like lunacy coming on the heels of that and all she could do to keep it away was to look at the boat and wait for Steve to reappear.

19

"Alarms are all blaring!"

Carl hoped they couldn't hear the pain in his voice. He thought he was hiding it pretty well. But the truth of the matter was that he was hurting like crazy. While the laptop was still secure and free of water—for the moment—Carl was beginning to experience minor shocks from everything else around him. He had no idea which equipment was responsible for them, but they were hitting him via the water. A few of them had been minor, nothing stronger than bee stings. But two had hit him hard, making him gasp and fear for his life.

"Carl, are you okay?"

This was Emily's voice. She sounded tired and concerned. Maybe he wasn't hiding the fact that he was in pain as well as he thought.

"Yeah, just wait for my word."

He used the controller to direct the third ROV to the Collector. He tried not to think about the shocks that could light him up at any moment. Instead, he focused on the thought of lining this last ROV up, switching on the pump, and getting the hell out of there.

As the ROV neared the Collector, the system on the laptop provided a warning in the form of a small flashing message on the screen: OBJECT APPROACHING. POSSIBLE INTERFERENCE.

Carl looked to the third ROV's camera and saw something huge approaching, darkening the glow of the small lights atop the rover.

"Okay, I see it coming!" Carl yelled. As he did, he was shocked yet again. This was a small one, but it lasted longer than the others. "I see it on the ROV cameras," he added, trying to distract himself. "It's coming in fast. Get to the raft now!"

He waded over to the side of the room, briefly losing his footing and nearly dropping the laptop into the water. It was up to his stomach now. He was already going to have to ditch the laptop to crawl back out of the cabin and onto the side of the boat. But if the water got any deeper—as in, more than three more inches—the water would start submerging the monitor he was using to operate the pump. If the damned shark didn't act fast, this was all for nothing.

From outside, he heard Emily scream Steve's name. She sounded scared and a little pissed. On the laptop screen, he saw the shark getting closer to the ROVs, their alarms still shrieking out underwater.

"Come on you bastard," Carl said through gritted teeth.

To his right, something made a popping noise. He looked over and saw that the wall (or, rather, what had once served as the floor) was buckling. He could see flickering lights under the murky water as a variety of electrical equipment displayed error lights.

"Hey man," came a voice from his left.

He turned and saw Steve. He was struggling to hold himself up by the frame where the window had once been. He was looking into the cabin and the shock on his face was apparent.

"Don't come in here," Carl said "I'm getting shocked every few seconds. Get outside and get in that raft."

"You coming with us?" Steve asked.

When Carl answered, it was the first time he had seriously felt the weight of the decision he had made. "Probably not." He looked back to the laptop screen and there was the megalodon, barreling towards the ROVs. "Go! I'm about to hit the pump. If I can make it out, I will. Just *go!*"

Steve nodded and said, "Good luck, man."

When the megalodon was inches away from the auxiliary cutter ROV, Carl gave it the command to turn on. The blades and diggers started up instantly. He then gave the same command to the others, but left them stationary, around the Collector. When the sediment and muck began to fly, Carl reached out to the monitor along the slanted console. He typed in the command to start the pump, just three simple buttons.

He was used to hearing the attachment alongside the boat start to hum when that command was entered but there was nothing now. The collector was working independently below him, sucking up debris and muck into nothing. A message popped up on the screen as water began to overtake it.

ATTACHMENT A-121 NOT ENABLED. PUMP SHUT DOWN?

Carl reached out and pressed **N** on the small keyboard beneath the monitor.

Behind him, there was another pop—this one like a firework. He turned to see what it was, but never got the chance.

He barely saw the small rack of computer equipment come sliding off of the wall. The external hard drives and other equipment he had never fully understood came crashing down into the water, already spitting out sparks. He saw the cables behind them, active and working, spilling out like guts into the water.

He felt the shock like a bullet as the current raced through the water and slammed into his body. This time, it did not let up. Carl's head rocked back as his body spasmed. He was unaware of the other popping and cracking noises from behind him. He was even barely able to see the laptop as he dropped it into the water.

Before he died, he took the smallest bit of gratification in the fact that the megalodon seemed to be fighting against the Collector as two of the three ROVs still stood upright, tearing into its flesh.

He even thought he saw its blood darkening the screen. It clouded up like mud from the bottom. He grinned in spite of himself. It was the best find the damned equipment had managed to come across all day

That was the last thing Carl saw as the current continued to tear through him. Even when he was dead, his body continued to tremble with the jolt as the boat continued to sink all around him.

20

Emily was both livid and hugely relieved when she saw Steve re-appear along the side of the boat. In the thirty or so seconds that had passed since he had gone down to check on Steve, it looked as if the boat had sunk another two feet or so. Seeing Steve, she realized that she had never even bothered to try getting the raft closer to the boat. Because it was an inflatable raft, there was nothing in the way of an oar or rope. The only accessory was a small blinking white light on the front of it. And being that the raft was pretty large—big enough to accommodate up to ten people if she had to guess—there was no way she could paddle it over by simply using her hand.

Apparently, Steve wasn't going to be stopped by such matters, though. She watched as he stepped to the edge and in the shades of night and the weak lights coming from the boat as well as the emergency light on the raft, she could see a new sort of determination in his face.

"Steve, are you sure—?"

He didn't bother with a response, not so much as a nod. He leaped off of the edge of the boat. His aim was great, as he headed directly for the raft, but his poise was not. He missed a clear landing by about two feet. His chest struck the outer edge of the raft and he bounced off, into the water. Emily was there at once, reaching out for him.

He grabbed her forearm and she pulled at once. When he was partially up, Steve caught on to the nylon straps around the raft's edge and pulled himself the rest of the way in. He slid over the edge of the raft and collapsed inside.

"Did it work?" Emily asked.

"I think so," he said.

"Well then where the hell is he?"

His frown said all that Emily needed to know. She looked back towards the boat and was surprised that they had seen it as any sort of safety. It was within just a few feet of sinking entirely and looked incredibly fragile.

"What do you think we should do?" Steve asked.

"I have no idea," Emily said. "If he's not about by now, then he's—"

The boat made a creaking noise loud enough to drown out her voice. This was followed by a snapping sound that must have caused serious structural damage; the boat rolled over ninety degrees and then started sinking at an angle.

"Oh God," Emily said. She wasn't sure what she was more distressed about—that the entire crew that had tried to kill them was now dead or that they were once again stranded out here in the sea.

"I think..." Steve said, but he closed his mouth and looked nearly embarrassed.

"What?"

"I think we'll be okay if we just stay quiet. Maybe if his plan worked, that thing is dead, you know?"

She nodded her head but she wasn't so sure. She had seen that hate and determination in that monster's dark eyes. To think that it had gone underwater to attack the rovers and would never again come to the surface was too much to hope for. Still, there was something to be said for Steve's brand of hope. It was calming, even in the face of uncertainty. She could do that...she could just lay here in the raft until they were rescued or swallowed whole by the megalodon. At this point, either one was fine with her. She just wanted this to be over.

"Emily?"

"Yeah?" she replied, feeling that she might be on the verge of crying again but finding it hard to muster up the strength to do so.

"Are you okay? Are you hurt?"

"No," she said, although she did have a vague memory of being trapped underwater, in the basket attached to the cable as the weight of it all had pulled her down. She couldn't help but wonder if things might have been better if the diver had not rescued her. At least death was a certainty. Being here, stranded at sea in the midst of a dark and cloudy night and not knowing if the megalodon was dead was somehow worse than death.

"You know more about the ocean than I do," Steve said. "What do we do now?"

"I don't know *anything* about rescuing stranded people at sea," she said, a little bitterly. "I think Carl was right before…we just have to wait to see if the Coast Guard comes back out to—"

A crashing sound from behind them cut her off and they both turned around screaming. There was water in that sound and Emily knew what it was at once. Even before her eyes took it in and saw the remainder of Carl's boat get dismantled, she knew.

It was the megalodon.

They turned just in time to see it breach, tearing through what remained of Carl's boat. It came up with tremendous force but there was something off about the way it moved. Once it was out of the water, it seemed to give up. Where it had come up out of the water like a rocket before, it now seemed to simply pop up and the crash back down.

It settled back into the water in a thrashing motion, as if it was hell-bent on making sure every single scrap of the boat was pummeled. Emily thought it looked a little like a child throwing a temper tantrum. She watched as it splashed and dipped and breached almost lazily among the wreckage.

That's when she actually took the time to look at the creature itself and not the destruction it was causing.

There were two enormous gouges along its head on the right side. One ran from the tip of its snout all the way down and around to the soft underside of its upper stomach. There was another one along its right fin but she was unable to see the complete damage, as much of it remained underwater. But it was the larger one along its head that seemed to be the worst of all. It was easily two feet wide and of a length that was hidden by the water. It came across the beast's eye, opening that black orb of evil even wider.

"His plan worked," Steve said quietly.

Emily nodded, slowly sitting back against the soft side of the raft. She knew that the helicopter pilot's blood was all around them but she didn't care in that moment. She watched the shark as it slowed its fit. It remained there in the midst of the debris for a while, going under for a moment and then coming back up. It was clearly out of sorts and in pain. It was odd, but seeing it in such a vulnerable state made it look even larger to Emily.

She reached out for Steve and took him by the arm as they watched the megalodon take one final plunge underwater. It made its movements slowly, flicking its tail almost playfully as it retreated under the water and out of sight.

They sat together, Emily's arm hooked through Steve's, as the small white emergency light at the head of the raft flashed into the dark like a dying star.

21

She saw the monster coming out of the water, its teeth like rows of glinting razors in its cavernous mouth. It roared when it surfaced and then it came directly for them. The menace was back in its eyes—even the one that had been shredded by Carl's rovers—and as Emily looked into that one good eye, she shared some sort of psychic connection with it.

I'm gonna get you now, bitch, it told her. *You're not going to get away from me this time.*

When it opened its mouth, she saw Zoe inside. Her face was a tattered mess of blood and skin. Muscle peeked through and when she smiled at her, maggots and worms wriggled out.

"You just let it eat me…"

She screamed.

The raft seemed to shudder around them and as the scream started to die in her throat, she heard Steve's voice. She was resting against him and he was cradling her. "Calm down," he told her. "You're okay. It was just a dream."

"I fell asleep?" she asked, surprised.

"Yeah."

"How long?"

Steve shrugged. "Twenty minutes, maybe. It's okay. Go back to sleep."

"No. I'm sorry. No…no sleep."

But God, she was tired.

She shook her head, finding the idea of sleeping in the midst of something like this ridiculous. She wasn't sure how the hell she had managed to fall asleep in the first place, considering everything she had just endured. She stared to the flickering little white light on the front of the raft and it seemed to hypnotize her. She thought of how the shark had looked when it had surfaced that last time. It had to be dead, right? It had nearly been torn to pieces. Or had the night and her exhausted state made it look worse than it had actually been?

She zoned out, slipping into a state between awake and asleep. She wondered if it was the trauma of it all, the horror of what she had seen and—

"Hey," Steve said.

"Huh?"

"Look."

She blinked, realizing that she had nearly fallen asleep again despite her attempts to stay somewhat alert. The raft bobbed along the ocean, rocked by its eternal arms. She wondered if solid ground would ever feel quite right beneath her feet again.

"What am I looking at?" she asked.

"Right there," Steve said, pointing up and to the left.

Emily looked up, squinting into the darkness of the sky. More clouds were gathered, probably bringing more rain. But the clouds weren't what Steve was pointing to. He was pointing to the light up there, the light that was growing larger by the second.

She sat up slowly, her eyes never leaving it. Within another ten seconds, she could hear a sound accompanying the light. It was a sound she'd heard in the last few hours—a sound she had mistakenly thought was the sound of being rescued.

She watched the light get closer, not taking her eyes away from it until she saw the clear shape of a helicopter form behind it. Further behind it, another light had appeared. She supposed that given the alarming nature of what had happened to the other crew, the Coast Guard had sent out two crews this time, just to be safe.

"We're going to be okay," Steve said. He was crying a bit and hearing it warmed Emily's heart.

Still, as the helicopter started to hover directly over them and a large whit spotlight was beamed down towards them, she still feared that she'd see that massive dorsal fin at any moment. Maybe it had been playing dead this whole time, waiting for a sense of hope in the humans it had been tormenting.

But there was no fin in the water around them. Even the remnants of the boats that they had both been on and seen destroyed were faint shapes in the water, left behind by the raft.

Emily watched a cable slowly descend from the helicopter and finally allowed herself to cry again. She wept into Steve's shoulder and did not stop until she felt the solid but shaky floor of the helicopter beneath her feet.

22

Four days later

Emily had been shocked to find that through everything that had happened in Carl's boat, Steve had suffered a broken left hand and a slight fracture in his left shoulder. Despite those things, he had done everything he could to help her and she had never noticed him favoring either of those injuries.

She had been informed of this when she'd been looked over in the hospital in Honolulu. Aside from a scratch on her right forearm and a migraine that seemed to not want to go away, she had come out of the whole ordeal relatively unscathed. She'd been cleared within twelve hours and had gone down to check on Steve.

Those first twenty-four hours after being rescued now felt like some extended episode of the horrors they had encountered out at sea. Emily tried to look back on them without feeling detached as they rode together in a cab to the airport. They were holding hands and she had no idea what that meant. She didn't see them going on any dates or anything when they got back home but— well, they had endured something horrific together and she knew that he had saved her life on at least two occasions. She was close to him in a way that she had never been close to a man before. She was not naïve enough to think it was love, but it made her feel secure, nonetheless.

The cab pulled up to the central airport entrance and they stepped out together. They walked inside and when the small group of people started coming towards them with cameras, it made no sense to Emily at first. But then the first of them started to ask questions—then a second and a third. It was not a massive crowd of reporters, but it was enough to be annoying. Emily had not been expecting such a crowd. She had been warned by one of the policemen that had guarded them at the hospital that some reporters had been snooping around, but Emily had never expected anything like this.

"What was it like to be face to face with a creature that most assumed to be nothing more than legend?" one woman asked.

"What can you tell me about the Coast Guard rescue?" asked another.

"Is there a blossoming romance between the two of you in the wake of this tragedy?"

"Will you ever go out onto a boat again?"

"Were you romantically involved with Cliff Zinsser?"

Emily thought about answering their questions but was simply not up for it. The idea of educating the public about a monster that was very much still alive when everyone that knew about it assumed it to be extinct was enticing. But at the same time, she was not ready to relive the horrors she'd witnessed. Not yet, anyway.

Steve gave her a look and nodded to her. She had no idea what he was trying to communicate so he took a stand that, quite frankly, impressed her.

He looked to them as sternly as he could, his hand in a cast and his shoulder braced with a sling. With the week or so of stubble on his face, he looked like a different person than the young man that had boarded a rented boat called *The Gull* six days ago mainly to spend time with a girl he had a massive crush on. Just by looking at him, you could tell that he had lived through something tragic.

"I'll answer your questions," he said in a loud and clear voice, "but please let Emily sit out. We've been through a lot. We're tired and out of sorts. Agreed?"

There was a chorus of agreement. Cameras angled to get a better shot of Steve and several microphones were thrust in front of him. Emily tiptoes away from it all, squeezing out the back of the group and ignoring the few questions people tried to hit her with despite their agreement with Steve.

She sat down against the far wall, watching people come and go. Some were in a hurry and others took their time. Some were alone, talking on cellphones, and others were in groups, scampering towards the food court or the baggage claim. It was amazing to her than none of these people knew about the prehistoric monster than now lay dead on the ocean floor thanks to Carl's quick thinking and classified machinery. They would live their lives not knowing about it, unless that caught some of Steve's answers on television.

After about fifteen minutes, Steve left the reporters, much to their chagrin. A few tried following him, but Steve then started to use expletives that seemed to keep them at bay. Emily took his hand again—rather proudly this time—and they headed for their gate.

When they arrived there, a single man began to approach them. There was a look of recognition in his eyes, but Emily had no idea who he was. He was an older man that looked joyful but a bit tired. Another reporter, probably.

"Are you Emily Nevins and Steve Locke?" the man asked.

"Who's asking?" Steve answered.

"My name is Corban Lyle," the man answered. "I worked with Cliff Zinsser quite a bit."

"I recognize the name," Emily said. "You did a lot of work with monk seals, right?"

"Yes. And I was, of course, very upset to hear about your ordeal."

There was a silence between them that Emily felt getting awkward right away. "So why are you here?" she asked.

"I was on the islands anyway, doing research on the preservation of monk seals and had to take this opportunity."

"Just to meet us?" Steve asked. "You're no better than the reporters."

"No…more than that," Corban said. "See, there are other areas on the oceans where there have been significant rises in the number of sperm and blue whale deaths. There is a particular area of interest off the coast of Papa New Guinea. Given the nature of the wounds, it is suspected that they are being killed by some unknown predator."

Emily felt that old familiar fear rising up but she pushed it down with unexpected anger. "Why are you telling me this?"

"Well…if it's…something like what you two have just faced…there is no one else on the planet that could give us insights into such a monster. You know how it moves, how it feeds, how it attacks."

"And?" Steve asked.

"Well," Corban said, looking to Emily with hope in his eyes. "What would your thoughts be on providing some information to those that need to know?"

"My thoughts?" Emily asked.

"Yes?"

"My thoughts are that you should leave it alone and let it eat." She saw those menacing black eyes in her mind, starting into her as if it could smell her fear. "Leave it alone and let nature run its course."

"But surely, you—"

"Goodbye, Mr. Lyle. My condolences for the loss of your friend."

"Yes, you too," Corban said, disappointed.

Emily took Steve by the hand again and headed for their gate.

The End

CHECK OUT OTHER GREAT
DEEP SEA THRILLERS

MEGA
by Jake Bible

There is something in the deep. Something large. Something hungry. Something prehistoric.
And Team Grendel must find it, fight it, and kill it.
Kinsey Thorne, the first female US Navy SEAL candidate has hit rock bottom. Having washed out of the Navy, she turned to every drink and drug she could get her hands on. Until her father and cousins, all ex-Navy SEALS themselves, offer her a way back into the life: as part of a private, elite combat Team being put together to find and hunt down an impossible monster in the Indian Ocean. Kinsey has a second chance, but can she live through it?

THE BLACK
by Paul E Cooley

Under 30,000 feet of water, the exploration rig Leaguer has discovered an oil field larger than Saudi Arabia, with oil so sweet and pure, nations would go to war for the rights to it. But as the team starts drilling exploration well after exploration well in their race to claim the sweet crude, a deep rumbling beneath the ocean floor shakes them all to their core. Something has been living in the oil and it's about to give birth to the greatest threat humanity has ever seen.

"The Black" is a techno/horror-thriller that puts the horror and action of movies such as Leviathan and The Thing right into readers' hands. Ocean exploration will never be the same."

CHECK OUT OTHER GREAT
DEEP SEA THRILLERS

PREDATOR X
by C.J Waller

When deep level oil fracking uncovers a vast subterranean sea, a crack team of cavers and scientists are sent down to investigate. Upon their arrival, they disappear without a trace. A second team, including sedimentologist Dr Megan Stoker, are ordered to seek out Alpha Team and report back their findings. But Alpha team are nowhere to be found – instead, they are faced with something unexpected in the depths. Something ancient. Something huge. Something dangerous. Predator X

DEAD BAIT
by Tim Curran

A husband hell-bent on revenge hunts a Wereshark...A Russian mail order bride with a fishy secret...Crabs with a collective consciousness...A vampire who transforms into a Candiru...Zombie piranha...Bait that will have you crawling out of your skin and more. Drawing on horror, humor with a helping of dark fantasy and a touch of deviance, these 19 contemporary stories pay homage to the monsters that lurk in the murky waters of our imaginations. If you thought it was safe to go back in the water...Think Again!

CHECK OUT OTHER GREAT DINOSAUR THRILLERS

THE VALLEY
by **Rick Jones**

In a dystopian future, a self-contained valley in Argentina serves as the 'far arena' for those convicted of a crime. Inside the Valley: carnivorous dinosaurs generated from preserved DNA. The goal: cross the Valley to get to the Gates of Freedom. The chance of survival: no one has ever completed the journey. Convicted of crimes with little or no merit, Ben Peyton and others must battle their way across fields filled with the world's deadliest apex predators in order to reach salvation. All the while the journey is caught on cameras and broadcast to the world as a reality show, the deaths and killings real, the macabre appetite of the audience needing to be satiated as Ben Peyton leads his team to escape not only from a legal system that's more interested in entertainment than in justice, but also from the predators of the Valley.

JURASSIC DEAD
by **Rick Chesler & David Sakmyster**

An Antarctic research team hoping to study microbial organisms in an underground lake discovers something far more amazing: perfectly preserved dinosaur corpses. After one thaws and wakes ravenously hungry, it becomes apparent that death, like life, will find a way.
Environmental activist Alex Ramirez, son of the expedition's paleontologist, came to Antarctica to defend the organisms from extinction, but soon learns that it is the human race that needs protecting.

CHECK OUT OTHER GREAT DEEP SEA THRILLERS

LAMPREYS
by Alan Spencer

A secret government tactical team is sent to perform a clean sweep of a private research installation. Horrible atrocities lurk within the abandoned corridors. Mutated sea creatures with insane killing abilities are waiting to suck the blood and meat from their prey.

Unemployed college professor Conrad Garfield is forced to assist and is soon separated from the team. Alone and afraid, Conrad must use his wits to battle mutated lampreys, infected scientists and go head-to-head with the biggest monstrosity of all.

Can Conrad survive, or will the deadly monsters suck the very life from his body?

DEEP DEVOTION
by M.C. Norris

Rising from the depths, a mind-bending monster unleashes a wave of terror across the American heartland. Kate Browning, a Kansas City EMT confronts her paralyzing fear of water when she traces the source of a deadly parasitic affliction to the Gulf of Mexico. Cooperating with a marine biologist, she travels to Florida in an effort to save the life of one very special patient, but the source of the epidemic happens to be the nest of a terrifying monster, one that last rose from the depths to annihilate the lost continent of Atlantis.

Leviathan, destroyer, devoted lifemate and parent, the abomination is not going to take the extermination of its brood well.

www.ingramcontent.com/pod-product-compliance
Lightning Source LLC
Chambersburg PA
CBHW022032170626
46808CB00003B/1158